A LITTLE HELP FROM
HIS FRIENDS

One of the thugs on Sullivan's trail shouted out to him, "You're pretty damned sure of yourself for someone alone in the jungle at night."

"I've got friends," Sullivan said. "Good buddies. Got one right here." He pulled the trigger of his M79 launcher and the grenade zoomed down the path like a flaring guided missile. The thugs didn't have time to wipe their noses before their blood and limbs were splashed over the trail. Three down. Maybe nineteen to go. . . .

In this book you will find a thrilling, danger-packed chapter from *The Beirut Retaliation*, the tenth novel in the exciting adventures of

THE SPECIALIST

Exciting Reading from SIGNET

THE SPECIALIST #9

VENGEANCE MOUNTAIN

John Cutter

A SIGNET BOOK

NEW AMERICAN LIBRARY

PUBLISHER'S NOTE

This novel is a work of fiction. Names, characters, places, and incidents either are the product of the author's imagination or are used fictitiously, and any resemblance to actual persons, living or dead, events, or locales is entirely coincidental.

NAL BOOKS ARE AVAILABLE AT QUANTITY DISCOUNTS WHEN USED TO PROMOTE PRODUCTS OR SERVICES. FOR INFORMATION PLEASE WRITE TO PREMIUM MARKETING DIVISION, NEW AMERICAN LIBRARY, 1633 BROADWAY, NEW YORK, NEW YORK 10019.

The first chapter of this book previously appeared in *One-Man Army*, the eighth volume in this series.

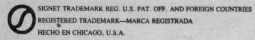

SIGNET TRADEMARK REG. U.S. PAT. OFF. AND FOREIGN COUNTRIES
REGISTERED TRADEMARK—MARCA REGISTRADA
HECHO EN CHICAGO, U.S.A.

SIGNET, SIGNET CLASSIC, MENTOR, PLUME, MERIDIAN and NAL BOOKS are published by New American Library, 1633 Broadway, New York, New York 10019

First Printing, June, 1985

1 2 3 4 5 6 7 8 9

PRINTED IN THE UNITED STATES OF AMERICA

1
The Stalkers

Jack Sullivan maneuvered the rented Cutlass into the exit lane, his eyes never leaving the two targets in their late-model midnight-blue Lincoln Continental. He'd followed them all the way from Manhattan, always careful to keep a few cars behind them. As he turned off the highway, a humorless smile creased his face. It shouldn't be long now, he thought.

This job had turned out to be surprisingly clean. He'd had time to plan, to stalk his targets and let them lead him to their den so he could complete the job in one attack. "Efficiency killing," Sullivan murmured to himself.

But as he drove down the tree-lined country road thirty yards behind the Lincoln, the smile faded from Sullivan's face. Rule Number One of the Specialist: Get cocky and get killed. Don't take anything for granted. There could be more to contend with than just these two slime buckets. No job is ever that neat.

The Lincoln came to a fork in the road and bore to the left without hesitating. Sullivan slowed to make it look like he was reading the sign, then took the road to the left, the road to Ashokan.

He'd been very careful not to blow his cover, but now

that they were the only two cars on the road, Sullivan had to be as inconspicuous as possible. That's why he had rented the white sedan and dressed in running shoes, jeans, a tan turtleneck, and a well-worn brown corduroy jacket. Just another suburban nature-lover out to see the fall foliage.

He glanced over to the navy-blue Cordura backpack on the seat next to him. Lunch.

Lake Williams stretched out to Sullivan's left, reflecting the golds and russets of the trees along its banks. The scum had picked some beautiful country for their dirty little operation. But Sullivan had long gotten used to the fact that parasites usually had pretty good taste when it came to picking a nest. No one ever suspects that something as ugly as a child-pornography operation could exist in such a beautiful place. It can't happen here. Yeah, right.

The blue Lincoln sped along the lake for about seven miles, then turned right onto a narrow road that cut into the woods. Sullivan pulled over and stopped by the lake for a minute before he turned down the road. He looked up at the chipped whitewashed road sign. Old Indian Road.

Sullivan knew he couldn't lose them on this deserted road, not if they were in a Lincoln. There were no houses, no side roads, just woods. After about a half-mile, Sullivan spotted a weather-beaten tin mailbox by the side of the road. Slowing down, he saw a narrow dirt drive overgrown with ferns. An old ramshackle house stood at the end of the drive. Its windows had been boarded up and part of the roof had caved in. It was a sharp contrast to the shiny new luxury sedan pulling around the back.

Bingo.

Sullivan pressed the accelerator and continued down the road another quarter-mile or so until he found a suitable copse of trees in which to hide his car. Switching off the ignition, he reached for the knapsack. He rummaged around in it then found what he was looking for. The .44 Auto-Mag emerged slowly from his knapsack like a cobra from a snake-charmer's basket.

Sullivan weighed the Auto-Mag in his hand. It was a very special weapon, without question the most powerful automatic pistol on the market. Its extra long 165mm barrel length gave it a sleek, snakelike profile, though it also made it cumbersome when carried under a jacket in a holster. Of course, this wasn't a problem for someone as large as Sullivan. He found a full clip in his backpack and slammed it into the weapon. It held eight cartridges, cartridges designed uniquely for the Automag—.44 revolver bullets fitted in cut-down 7.62mm NATO rifle cartridge cases. The manufacturer listed it as a hunting weapon, and that's just what Sullivan was using it for. Hunting.

He got out of the car, tucked the Auto-Mag into his belt, slung the backpack over his shoulder, and disappeared into the woods, heading for his quarry.

Preminger peered through field glasses from his perch in a tree behind the dilapidated house. He'd staked out the house days ago, and this was the second boring afternoon he'd spent waiting for the attack. It was a relief to see Babcock's blue Lincoln pull into the drive. For one thing, it relieved the incredible monotony of watching the squirrels watching him; for another, Preminger would finally get to see the kiddie-porn king in the flesh, Harry Babcock.

But when Babcock rolled out from behind the wheel of the Lincoln, Preminger was disappointed. He'd expected a flashy dude with dark wavy hair, a pearly smile, and an Italian-cut silk suit. Sort of a sleazy Victor Mature type. What emerged from the car was an overweight bald guy in his early fifties wearing a thick gray cardigan sweater and round gold-rimmed glasses. His brows had a sympathetic slant and he looked totally harmless—sort of a smutty Mr. Rogers.

Babcock's bodyguard was more in character, though. Greasy black hair, dangling cigarette, butternut leather

trench coat, pointy gray suede shoes. From the unpro-
fessional way he held open the front of his coat, he
might as well have worn a sign that read I'M CARRYING A
CANNON.

After Babcock and his bodyguard went into the house
through the cellar hatch, Preminger scanned the nearby
woods. He spotted movement. He focused his glasses
and saw a pair of huge shoulders and a dark head of
hair with white-streaked sideburns moving carefully
toward the house. Preminger watched the man stalk up
to the side of the house and peer through the windows
on the ground floor.

"Well, if it isn't the Specialist," Preminger murmured
to himself. "Okay, Sullivan, let's see what you can do."

Babcock hit the lights in the basement of the shabby
house, illuminating his newest studio. Instead of the
gloomy, cobweb-ridden cellar the old house should have
had, it had wall-to-wall carpeting and expensive high-
tech furnishings. One end of the room hosted a lounge
complete with a fully stocked bar, plush sofas, and a
six-foot video projection screen. At the other end was
the work area where the movies were made. A big
black movie camera sat on the tripod like a giant spider
staring dead-eyed at the set—a double bed on a plat-
form spread with red satin sheets. The backdrop was a
screen painted to resemble a kid's bedroom with a toy
shelf on the wall and frilly curtains on the painted
windows.

"Hey, this is some setup you got here, Mr. Babcock,"
the bodyguard marveled as he came down the cellar
steps.

"Close the cellar door behind you, Lenny. And lock
it." Babcock didn't want anyone getting in or out when
he worked.

Babcock sorted through his key ring as he went into
the other part of the cellar, the part where the coal bin
used to be. The walls in this room were lined with

floor-to-ceiling shelving full of videotapes and film canisters. His inventory of kiddie-porn films. His specialty.

He walked up to a steel door that sealed off what used to be the coal bin and unlocked the dead bolt. A dim light from within spilled out into the basement as Babcock peered in to check on his latest star. A little girl, no more than ten years old, gazed at Babcock through the tangled strands of her golden blond hair. She sat trembling on a narrow bed, her legs tucked underneath her. She was completely naked.

"I told you I'd come back, didn't I?" Babcock said with a reassuring smile.

The little girl didn't respond, but Babcock was used to this kind of behavior from his leading ladies. He stepped over the dolls and board games strewn over the floor and opened the half-size refrigerator. "Ran out of food, I see. I didn't think a little sweetie like you could eat that much. Well, it's better that you're a little hungry. You work better when you're hungry, did you know that? First we'll do a little work and then we can have some cookies and milk. How does that sound?"

Babcock had a knack for making whatever he said sound warm and reassuring to a child. Some would say he had a natural way with kids. That's how he got his stars to do what no other pornographer had ever gotten children to do on film. You name it, Babcock had filmed it. Even kiddie snuff porn.

And if his little actors and actresses didn't like the script ... well, Babcock just disciplined them. Very severely.

"Come on, sweetie. It's showtime." Babcock took the little girl by the hand and led her out to the set. Scared out of her wits, she followed like a zombie.

"Aw-right!" Lenny yelled from the sofa where he'd settled in with a double Scotch. "A little tits and ass, and I do mean little."

"Shut up, Lenny!" Babcock snapped. "I don't put up with distractions when I work. Isn't that right, Melinda?" His tone had changed instantly from venomous to sugary when he addressed the little girl.

"Sorry, Mr. Babcock. I'll be quiet."

"See to it that you are."

Babcock led the little girl to the big bed and told her to get up. He then went to his "prop department," a corner of the basement cluttered with boxes and racks of negligees, corsets, and sequined gowns all in various child sizes. He dug through one of the boxes and came up with what he was looking for. A twelve-inch baby-pink dildo.

"Okay, Melinda," he said, holding out the dildo to the little girl like a lollipop. "Now, if you really want those cookies we were talking about, all you have to do is—"

Everything suddenly went black. The lights had gone out. Melinda screamed in terror, and Lenny started to curse.

"Damn," Babcock spat. "Lenny, listen to me. There's a flashlight behind the bar. Get it so we can find the fuse box."

The bodyguard was still cursing under his breath as he reached into his pocket for his butane lighter. He flicked his Bic and nearly pissed his pants when he saw the killer eyes set deep in the grim scarred face eerily lit from below, an executioner's face looming right in front of him.

"Shit!" Lenny yelped as he fumbled for his piece, but the Specialist beat him to the draw. The strobe flash from the Auto-Mag lit the room for a split second as Sullivan blew the greaseball away at point-blank range, the 7.62mm slug ripping through his breastbone to make hash of his heart before smashing out his back. Lenny's guts and blood splashed messily on the wall behind him.

In the darkness, Sullivan heard Babcock's stumbling footsteps on the wooden stairway that led to the first floor. Remembering the layout of the room, Sullivan leapt over a sofa and dashed up the steps after the pornographer. He caught up with the huffing fat man

in the dusty upstairs hallway and brought him down by
smashing Babcock's head with the butt of his gun.

Sullivan unslung his backpack as he looked down at
the heap of blubber on the dirty floor. He unzipped a
side pocket and pulled out a pair of handcuffs, then
gathered up Babcock's wrists and bound them behind
his back.

"Don't go away," Sullivan said as he shoved the
Auto-Mag in his belt, went back downstairs, and headed
to the fuse box in a corner opposite the set.

Switching on the lights, he saw the little girl clutching
the obscene satin sheets, shivering in fear. Sullivan started
to say something, but then decided against it. Babcock
had conned this poor kid with his Mr. Gentle routine,
so she sure wouldn't trust him if he came on to her the
same way.

"Hi," he said casually, walking slowly toward her.
"Are you cold? You look cold."

The girl didn't answer. The long scar across Sullivan's right cheek from his eye to his jawline frightened
her. He was an imposing figure, standing more than
six feet tall, and his massive build filled the small set.

Sullivan opened his backpack and pulled out a small
orange jumpsuit and a pair of leather-soled slipper
socks. "Here," he said, tossing them onto the bed. "You
can have these." He didn't want to approach her until
he was sure he had her confidence.

He reached into his pack and came up with something wrapped in aluminum foil. Melinda stared at him
in curiosity. He unwrapped it, then made a face. "Peanut butter and jelly again? I hate peanut butter and
jelly. Do you want it?"

Sullivan held out the sandwich and stepped forward.
She reached out for the food in desperation. From the
way she devoured it, it was clear she hadn't eaten in
days.

Melinda let him help her on with the clothes as she
finished the sandwich. Next he produced a box of

animal crackers. He opened the box, popped one in his mouth, then handed the rest to Melinda.

"I don't like this place," he said, looking around. "In fact, I *hate* this place. I'm going. You want to come?"

Melinda nodded, her mouth full, her blue eyes as big as saucers.

Sullivan picked her up, and immediately she threw her arms around his neck. "It's okay, Melinda," he said softly. "The nightmare is over."

He brought her upstairs, covering her eyes so she wouldn't have to see Babcock, who was just coming around. Gently Sullivan lowered her out the same window he'd used to come in. "Now, Melinda, you wait over there by that big tree, okay? I'll be out in a minute."

Melinda nodded and did as he asked.

"Hey . . . hey you! What the fuck do you think you're doing?" Babcock shouted. "Where's my kid?"

"*Your* kid?" Sullivan said, grabbing Babcock by the collar and dragging him back downstairs like a sack of potatoes.

Babcock yelped when he saw the six-inch hole in his bodyguard's chest. Blood and shreds of organs were splattered all over his nice pastel-colored lounge.

"I suppose in a way they were all your kids, Babcock. That's the scam, right? You adopt homeless kids, then put 'em to work in your porno flicks. If they don't cooperate, they don't eat. And if they still don't play ball, then they get beaten."

"No, no, you got me wrong, man," Babcock blithered. "I just do soft-core stuff. Honest. I don't hurt them."

"Sure, tell me another one."

Babcock squirmed helplessly as Sullivan dragged him to the back room where the films and cassettes were stored. Sullivan stood him up and shoved him against the shelves. Babcock's nose smashed against the edge of one shelf; then he fell into a heap, videotapes raining down around him.

"Hey, come on, man," Babcock pleaded. "Take it easy."

Sullivan ignored him while he read some of the titles printed on the spines of the video cassette boxes. "Let's see what you've got here—*Babes in Toyland . . . Dick and Jane Have a Ball . . . Bang-Bang, You're Dead . . . Lassie, Come Home. . . .*" Sullivan bounced the films off Babcock's belly as he read the titles.

"Look, man, you're destroying my inventory. Name your price. Just tell me what the fuck you want."

"I'm already being paid, Babcock. Paid to hang up your ass."

"What . . . ?"

"Don't look so surprised, Babcock. Do you remember a little girl named Ginger Hayes? You must remember her. She's the reason you had to leave California and set up shop here in New York."

"I don't know what the hell you're talking about." The sweat streaming down Babcock's fat face indicated otherwise.

"Let me refresh your memory. One day you picked up the paper and read about this couple in Sausalito who died in a suicide pact. They had a little girl, seven years old. The paper said there were no surviving relatives and the kid had to go to a foster home. Perfect kid for you, you figured, so you adopted her, became her legal guardian. You'd done that number before plenty of times. The adoption agencies in California actually thought you were a real prince, taking all these kids in. Man, did you ever have them buffaloed."

"You've got the wrong guy. That's not me," Babcock whimpered.

"It's you, all right. That 'script girl' you sent out to dispose of the body testified to it. She got cold feet and ran to the police. I've seen the pictures of Ginger's body. What did you use on her? A rubber truncheon?"

"Noooo," Babcock whined. "Let me explain—"

"No, let me explain it to you, Babs. Or should I say Henry Bucknell? That's the name you were using when you offed Ginger Hayes. See, what you didn't know was that Ginger's father had a brother in Alaska. Yeah, and when Uncle Dave got wind of what you did to his niece, he got pretty crazy. Uncle Dave's one of those rugged mountain types, so he wasn't about to let the law deal with you. He knows that guys like you have a way of slipping away from justice. That's why he hired me to do the job."

Sullivan dug into his backpack and came up with some nylon clothesline, which he used to tie Babcock to one of the uprights of the shelves bolted to the wall. Babcock blubbered like an infant as Sullivan opened one film canister after another and dumped them on the porno king. When Babcock was up to his chest in spilled film and cassettes, Sullivan went back to his bag and pulled out a two-quart thermos bottle.

"Uncle Dave told me his one wish is that you should burn in hell. And since you store your masters and your inventory right here, we can make Uncle Dave's dream come true and get rid of your whole dirty operation in one neat package."

Sullivan unscrewed the top of the thermos bottle, releasing blue gasoline fumes. He calmly splashed gas on top of the mountain of porn, then tossed the thermos aside. Reaching into his inside pocket, Sullivan took out a pack of Lucky Strikes and stuck one between his lips.

"Uncle Dave will be very happy," Sullivan muttered, making the unlit cigarette jump.

Ignoring the screaming man on the floor, Sullivan lit his cigarette and tossed the burning match behind him as he left. He heard the *phoomp* of the gas igniting and the piercing screams of the condemned man. Sullivan's only worry was that Melinda might hear the screams outside. She'd already gone through enough.

Little Melinda took Sullivan's hand and followed him through the woods back to his car. She didn't seem to be afraid of him, but Sullivan hoped her trust wasn't based solely on a food bribe. A lot of people believed that trust only got you into trouble, but Sullivan couldn't

disagree more. If you couldn't put your trust in someone, something in life, you might as well be dead. He
just hoped to God that Melinda's experience with that
slime Babcock hadn't done any permanent damage and
hardened her soul for good.

But as they strolled through the orange-gold leaves
covering the ground, something interrupted Sullivan's
train of thought. He sensed it instinctively before
he actually heard anything. It was a sixth sense he'd
picked up in Nam when he'd led lurps deep into
Viet Cong territory. Lurps—long-range reconnaissance
patrols—were basically suicide missions, jungle hikes to
"Camp Dead Dog," because once you got out of radio
range of your base camp, you could forget about calling for helicopter support if you got into a jam. All you
had on lurps was what you and your men carried on
their backs. If you stood any chance of surviving a
long-range mission, you had to find the enemy before
they found you. One of the Specialist's specialties was
this gift he had for sensing enemy presence even in the
thickest jungle. That's how he'd been able to run count-
less lurp missions and always come back to tell about
them.

He sensed somebody tracking him right now.

They kept walking, Sullivan smiling at Melinda, pre-
tending that his guard was down and that he didn't
suspect a thing. But his mind was working like a computer, sizing up the terrain, measuring distances, weigh-
ing the options and the risks. As Sullivan saw it, there
were two imperatives: getting the girl out of harm's
way and not tipping his hand too soon.

When they got to the car, Sullivan opened the passenger door and let Melinda in. He unslung the blue
backpack from his shoulder, reached in, and pulled out
another thermos bottle.

"What's that?" Melinda asked.

Sullivan looked at her, then looked at the thermos
clutched in his fist. "Chocolate milk," he said. "You like
chocolate milk, don't you?"

Melinda nodded eagerly.

"Okay, this is for you, then. Save a little for me, though."

"Okay." She smiled.

"Say, Melinda, will you do me a favor? See that lever right there?" He pointed to the hood release under the dashboard. "Pull that lever for me, okay?"

"Okay."

Sullivan went around to the front of the car and lifted the hood.

Preminger couldn't see the Specialist from where he was crouched behind a stand of tall ferns. His view was blocked by the raised hood of the Cutlass. What the hell is he doing? Preminger wondered. Then it occurred to him that the car might be equipped with a hidden kill switch that cut off the ignition and prevented the engine from starting. Lots of people had them in their cars to guard against theft; Preminger didn't give it a second thought.

He relaxed his grip on the .44 Bulldog in his hand. He had no intention of tangling with the Specialist, but from what he'd heard, the guy could be a maniac. He had heard the bloodcurdling screams from the old house, and there was no doubt in his mind that Sullivan was lethal, so a little caution was in order. But what the hell was he doing under the hood so—

And then Preminger had only darkness to contemplate.

When he came to, he was flat on his back trying to focus his eyes. Two looming shapes standing over him finally came together. It was the imposing form of Jack Sullivan emptying the cartridges out of Preminger's revolver.

While Preminger thought Sullivan was fiddling under the hood of the car, the Specialist had slipped back into the woods, circled around behind "the enemy," coldcocked him, and disarmed him. Tossing the empty gun aside, Sullivan bent his knees and tensed his hands.

The grim look in Sullivan's eyes warned Preminger that if he tried something stupid, the Specialist could break him in half with his bare hands.

"Who are you and why are you following me?" Sullivan growled. "And remember—you lie, you die."

Preminger rubbed the back of his head but wisely didn't try to sit up. "My name's Preminger. I'm a private detective."

"Yeah? What else?"

"I was hired by a group of people who want to engage your services. They heard your fee is pretty steep, so they wanted to have you checked out before they put up that kind of cash. Some of them were skeptical about your reputation. They hired me to find out firsthand how effective you really are." Preminger rotated his head and winced with pain. "I'd say you're pretty fucking effective."

Sullivan didn't say a word; his gaze never wandered from his captive. His inner computer was racing, analyzing this Preminger. Private dicks come in all colors, he reasoned. Just like everything else, there are good ones, bad ones, and useless ones. Preminger had to have balls to take this assignment, but there was something unmistakably shady about him. Still, Sullivan's gut feelings told him that Preminger was telling the truth now.

"What exactly do your clients want me to do for them?"

"They want vengeance. There are twenty-nine people in this group, and they all lost someone close to them. All murdered by the same killer."

Sullivan didn't have to hear any more. In his mind, he was already on the job.

2
Safe Harbor

"You have an office, I assume?" Sullivan asked.

"In Manhattan. West Thirty-Eighth Street—"

"Call your clients and arrange a meeting. I'll be in touch."

Preminger sat up and shook his head as he watched the Specialist heading back to his car. He heard the Cutlass roar to life and his splitting head started to throb.

Shoulda charged more for this goddamn job, Preminger thought angrily.

Melinda was slumped against Sullivan's shoulder, fast asleep, as he carried her up the three flights of stairs to Bonnie Roland's apartment on the Upper West Side of Manhattan. The kid had been exhausted to begin with, and the ride down to the city knocked her right out. Sleep like this was a way of forgetting, and Melinda had a lot of forgetting to do. Sullivan gently shifted her head so she'd be more comfortable on his rock-hard shoulder.

Standing in front of Bonnie's door, Sullivan dug into his pants pocket for the key she'd given him. It was easy to locate on his key ring because it was the only two-pronged cylinder key he had, and the sight of it made his stomach burn. That key fit into the special four-way lock system Bonnie had installed, a system guaranteed to deter a break-in of any kind for at least as long as it took to escape out the window. The fact that Bonnie had to take such measures to live in peace in her own home aggravated the hell out of Sullivan.

But when he swung open the door and saw Bonnie Roland lying on the sofa engrossed in a book, his outrage dissipated. He quietly watched her for a moment, taking in her long loose strawberry-blond hair, her dazzling cat-green eyes, her long shapely legs clad in skin-tight jeans, her perfect, inviting skin. Bonnie sometimes had a calming effect on Sullivan.

He couldn't help wondering if he was putting Bonnie in danger by his mere proximity. He had plenty of enemies, and anyone near him could easily get caught in the crossfire.

Bonnie put down her book and was about to say something when she spotted Melinda sleeping in Sullivan's arms. From the instant panic in her eyes, Sullivan could tell what she was thinking—the kid's dead.

"Jack," Bonnie said in a husky whisper, "who . . . what . . . ?"

"Her name is Melinda," he said. "She'll be okay . . . I think."

"What happened to her?" There was a pained expression on Bonnie's face.

"She was held captive by a porno filmmaker. He was forcing her to 'act' in his movies. But she won't have to worry about him anymore."

Bonnie got up from the sofa to get a closer look at the child. "It doesn't look like he beat her."

"They never beat them unless they really have to. Bruised kids don't make pretty actresses. She is hurt, though. Inside her head."

Sullivan put Melinda down on the sofa where Bonnie had been, and covered her with a brown-and-tan afghan. Bonnie realized that Sullivan needed a drink. She went to the kitchen and poured him three fingers of Dewar's straight up. Sullivan followed her in and took the glass gratefully. He killed off most of it in one gulp.

"What are you going to do with her, Jack?" Bonnie asked.

Sullivan was silent for a moment. "I've been asking myself that question all afternoon. She's a pretty tough kid to have survived what she's been through. I thought about finding a good foster home for her, but that's how she fell in with the pornographer in the first place."

"Forget about the city agencies," Bonnie said, shaking her head. "Every day I read in the paper about kids getting molested and raped by the staff creeps at the adoption facilities. Those places are snake pits."

"I know," Sullivan murmured, pouring himself another drink. "Tell me something—you ever hear of a private dick named Preminger?"

"Russ Preminger? I know a little bit about him."

"What?"

"Well, he's good. High marks on results, but low on loyalty. He goes with the highest bidder, no matter what, and it's not unlike him to switch sides in the middle of a case if the other side ups his fee. I've gotten a few of his disgruntled ex-clients. But why are you interested in him?" She twined her slender arms around his neck and nestled into his massive chest. "If you're in the market for a private eye, why not hire me?"

Sullivan pulled her close and regarded her with half-closed eyes. "Oh, I'd always think of you first if I needed a good detective. Preminger approached me. He was checking me out for some clients of his. Seems they need a merc to do a number on a psycho."

"Are you going to take the job?" Bonnie looked worried.

"I don't know yet. I've got to talk to the clients first." He could read the concern written on her face, so he changed the subject. "What worries me now is Melinda.

You wouldn't consider taking her in, at least for a while, would you?"

"Me? I'm not exactly the motherly type."

"You don't have to be a mother to her, just a friend."

Bonnie looked into his eyes. She could sense that there was more to his suggestion than he was saying.

"Since the foster homes are such treacherous shitholes, I was thinking maybe we could keep her."

"You mean adopt her? You and me?"

"Well, something like that. Think about it."

Bonnie's eyes glistened as she looked from Sullivan to the sleeping child on her sofa. Melinda represented something Bonnie thought she'd never have—a concrete link with the elusive Jack Sullivan. Could he actually be staking his claim with her? Bonnie hoped, but didn't dare put it into words.

Inside, Sullivan was pleased by Bonnie's reaction. He knew that Melinda would be safe with her. And who knows? Maybe deep down he did want something a little more permanent with Bonnie.

"The kid's sacked out," he finally said. "She'll probably be out for a couple of hours."

"That's exactly what I was thinking." Bonnie's voice was low, hungry, and sultry as she ran her hot-red fingernails over his hairy chest.

"Want to kill some time together?" he asked with a grin.

"I thought you'd never ask." A mischievous grin played on her lips as she started unbuttoning her blouse.

His hand crept around her waist as they headed for the bedroom, careful to close the door very quietly behind them.

3

Angel of Vengeance

The meeting took place in Preminger's office late that Friday afternoon. The muffled sound of bumper-to-bumper traffic—commuters battling to get through the Lincoln Tunnel and get a jump on the weekend—provided a background of white noise to the proceedings.

Once upon a time Preminger's office had been nicely decorated, but neglect had gotten the better of it. The carpet was stained, the two oatmeal couches were getting nappy, the chrome-and-glass coffee table was tarnished and smudged, and all the plants were long dead. Sullivan's lean bulk took up half of one couch. The three representatives of the aggrieved families sat facing him on the other couch. Preminger perched behind his desk with his feet in a bottom drawer. He did most of the talking for the organization.

Sullivan only half-listened. The intense look in the young brunette's dark eyes told him all he needed to know. It was a look Sullivan knew very well, the gnawing, pressure-cooker look of someone who's seen gross injustice. There was only one cure for that malady—vengeance.

". . . his name is Faraday, Jerome Faraday. A class-A wackerino, a psycho killer right out of the movies, a rabid misogynist. This perv has killed 180 women and teenage girls that we know of. He's certainly capable of having done many more. Most of the families of the murdered women refused to take part in any private vigilante action, for financial reasons, fear of prosecution for taking the law into their own hands, or fear of reprisal from Faraday. My clients represent twenty-nine of the victims. To put it simply, Sullivan, they're prepared to pay you two hundred thousand dollars cash to put Faraday away."

Sullivan's jaw was solid rock clenched in anger and outrage. "Why the hell haven't the police nabbed him? They've had 180 fucking chances."

"This guy is slippery. He never leaves an MO because he never strikes the same way twice. Sometimes he'd do a real sicko number, hacking up the body like chicken parts. Other times he tried to make it look accidental, household mishaps and stuff, like listening to the radio in the tub or falling down a flight of stairs. Some killings were short and sweet—bullet in the head, icepick in the spine; others were prolonged, days of torture, heavy bondage, S&M rituals."

Sullivan looked at the three people on the couch across from him. He could see the young guy's temples throbbing, and the well-dressed middle-aged lady was silently crying, reliving her own tragedy. But the brunette remained the same, her smoldering eyes boring into Sullivan's skull.

"How about the Bureau?" Sullivan asked. "Couldn't they help?"

"Yeah, as a matter of fact, the FBI finally picked up Faraday in St. Louis after he offed a girl who worked at a Burger King. The scum babbled a long confession, but as rotten luck would have it, the bureau car was broadsided by a pickup truck on the way to Faraday's arraignment. It was a bad crash; one of the agents died. Faraday escaped in the confusion."

"Any idea where he is now?"

"I have pretty good reason to believe he's in Florida. An agent I use down there spotted him in Boca Raton.

It could just be a coincidence, but there's a possibility
that he ran to his father for help. I tend to doubt it,
though, because Faraday hasn't been on speaking terms
with his old man since 1976. But if Faraday Senior is
hiding his son, we could have trouble."

"What kind of trouble?"

"Jerome Faraday Senior is the president, CEO, and
chairman of the board of Faraday International. It's an
industrial empire, Sullivan. Oil, steel, rubber, corporate
farming, telecommunications, real estate, precious metals, everything. He literally has money to burn. With
his old man's resources, Junior will be very tough to
find, let alone get close to. On the bright side, though,
I seriously doubt that the old man would take his kid in
after all these years. He's supposed to be a hard-hearted
old bastard, ruthless, and as stubborn as they come."

Sullivan grunted at Preminger's theories; he'd make
his own assessments.

"Mr. Sullivan," the young man, Brad Lucas, finally
piped up, "we've done a lot of research, investigated a
lot of your colleagues—if that's what you call them—
and the overwhelming consensus is that you're the best.
Despite what Mr. Preminger says about Faraday's father's money and power, we believe that you can get
him, wherever he is. He killed my wife, Mr. Sullivan.
Do you want to know how? Well, I'm a carpenter, see?
I have a lot of power tools—circular saw, routers, sand-
ers, jigsaw, stuff like that. That monster cornered my
wife in my shop, Mr. Sullivan." Lucas's face was red, his
voice straining and cracking. "He used them all, Mr.
Sullivan. Every goddamn tool I owned."

The middle-aged woman wiped her eyes and straight-
ened the neat bow of her silk blouse. Looking closer,
Sullivan could see that she wasn't as old as he originally
thought. The deep lines around her mouth and the
gray in her soft brown hair were premature. Just like
the white streaks in his own hair. The woman wasn't
much more than thirty-five.

She cleared her throat, struggling to hold back her

tears. "It was my daughter, Mr. Sullivan. He kidnapped her, held her captive in a shack in the Berkshires for over a week, the police said. He raped her, Mr. Sullivan, raped her in every way you could imagine. They found her naked body lashed to a tree . . . partially devoured by raccoons. My Megan was ten years old, Mr. Sullivan," she sobbed. "Get him . . . get him for Megan!"

Rage started collecting at the base of Sullivan's neck, the kind of rage that turned him into a killing machine. Ten years old, he thought. Same age as Melinda.

He looked to the young brunette, waiting to hear her story, but she didn't say a word, didn't move a muscle. She was young, college age, lithe and muscular, maybe a marathoner or a gymnast . . . or a black-belt. Her dark eyes were still locked on his, and he could feel the hate stored up inside her radiating out like heat from a wood stove.

"Ah, this is Angela Mills," Preminger finally said, breaking the awkward silence. "Her mother was—"

"My mother was unrecognizable," Angela interrupted sharply. "If it wasn't for her dental records, we wouldn't have known it was her." The cold hate in her voice chilled the room. "The New York *Post* called her the Hamburger Lady."

Sullivan's heart was pounding. He wished he had his hands around this Faraday's throat right now. But he forced himself to calm down. He had to have all the facts before he started anything.

"You had him spotted in Boca, Preminger. Why didn't you have your man do the job?" Sullivan asked.

"Not my line of work. I run a strictly legit agency here."

"Yeah, so I hear," Sullivan muttered.

Suddenly Angela Mills stood up and shouted, "Let's cut the shit, okay? Are you gonna do it or not?"

Sullivan locked eyes with her again, standing slowly to unfold his full impressive height. "I'll get him." He nodded. "I'll get him for you . . . or die trying."

4

Going to See a Man About a Psycho

Special Agent Sanson sat in the corner booth of a Greek coffee shop on West Fourteenth Street, smoking, glancing at his watch, waiting. Sullivan was late.

The waitress came by and refilled his coffee cup without asking. She assumed he was a salesman of some kind, just killing time between appointments. He sort of looked like a salesman—navy-blue polyester suit, regimental striped tie, close-cropped steel-gray hair. What she didn't notice were his vigilant, cool blue eyes and the bulge under his left armpit. To those in the know, Sanson was a picture-perfect fed, one of the Bureau's best.

He glanced at his watch again, then scanned the street outside the window. Seasoned agents got to be experts on waiting—sitting tight on stakeouts—and Sanson was prepared to wait it out for Sullivan. This time he needed the Specialist's services as much as the Specialist needed the information Sanson had to offer.

Finally, at a quarter to four, Sanson spotted Jack Sullivan crossing Fourteenth Street, approaching the coffee shop. Sullivan pushed through the door, his eyes already riveted on Sanson. Neither man smiled or greeted the other in any conventional way. They didn't have to. Sullivan went directly to Sanson's booth and slid into the opposite seat, his brown leather jacket squeaking against the vinyl upholstery.

Sullivan spotted the file folder on the white Formica tabletop, stuffed thick as the Manhattan phone directory. "Did I hit the lottery?" he asked wryly. Whenever Sanson offered information, it was always selective. Total access to FBI files was unprecedented for the Specialist.

"Faraday's a bad egg," Sanson said evenly. "We want him dead as much as anyone."

"So why don't you guys do it yourself?"

"Can't. But I'll get to that in a minute." He pushed the folder to Sullivan. "Most of this stuff is police paperwork on the murders—testimonies, detectives' reports, coroners' reports, the usual. It'll give you a pretty good idea why we want him out of the picture."

"I've heard as much as I need to know. You don't have to convince me that this guy needs a bullet in the head."

"Fine. What I've also included here is everything *we* have on Faraday. I'm sticking my neck out letting you in on this, but I have a feeling you can use it better than we can. Basically, we know that Faraday's father is protecting him, and that poses problems."

"I heard that they hated each other's guts, that Faraday Senior had disowned his little Jerome."

Sanson shook his head. "Not so. See, Faraday Senior isn't too stable himself. All his money has gone to his head, I guess, and he thinks that his family is some kind of American royalty. Protecting his family name is all-important to him. That's why he's protecting his son. Faraday Senior sees his son's murder spree as a minor indiscretion, simply an annoying bad habit that could mar the Faraday name if Jerome was ever caught and convicted."

"So why can't you guys get to him if you know where he is?"

"Father and son have split for Mexico, the Yucatán. Faraday Senior has a mansion in the jungle there. Ac-

tually it's a refurbished Spanish fortress on a mountain-
top surrounded by dense tropical jungle. I won't tell
you the place is impregnable, but the word has been
used to describe it. We also know that they've hired a
bunch of local thugs to patrol the place, at least twenty
of them. Our assumption is that Faraday Senior is
running the show now—as long as Junior behaves himself, Daddy will protect him."

Sullivan flipped through the file. "You still haven't
told me why you guys can't get to him."

"Political problems. Faraday Senior is very chummy
with the Mexican authorities. He's got them all paid
off. We've tried to extradite Jerome, but the locals
naturally won't cooperate. The other branch planned
to go in with an assassination squad, but the guys upstairs nixed that. The government's taken a lot of heat
for covert CIA operations in Central America. If they
got caught in Mexico, our supposed friend south of the
border, the shit would hit the fan internationally. That's
why I've come to you. Unofficially you have the Bureau's blessing to do whatever you have to in order to
put Faraday out. Of course, we can't give you men or
weapons, but whatever info we get will be passed on to
you. If you get caught, though, we'll disavow any knowledge of your operation."

"In other words, I'm dead meat on a tortilla."

Sanson smiled for the first time that week. "In a
manner of speaking, yes."

Sullivan continued to flip through the file until he
came to the pictures of Jerome Faraday Jr. The first
one was an eight-by-ten of his college-yearbook picture.
On the back was written "Yale, class of '68." In another
picture, Faraday was seated on top of a horse with a
polo mallet in his hand. In the last picture, he was
leaning on the fender of a jet-black BMW 318i, a straw
hat tilted jauntily on his head. Sullivan studied his
features, and the bile rose in his throat. Instead of the
bloated, fish-belly-white geek he had expected, Faraday
was an Ivy League dreamboat—tall and slender, neat

dirty-blond hair artfully mussed, violet-blue eyes, long lashes, thin nose, perfect smile. All Izod shirts, Top-Siders, and blue blazers.

That old familiar rage started rolling through Sullivan's brain. This guy was born with the proverbial silver spoon in his mouth, had everything money could buy, never had to work a day in his life—but just for kicks, he killed women. No doubt there was some psychological reason why he was sexually warped—repressed homosexuality, hatred of his mother, something like that. Even if he was caught and went to trial, his old man would hire the craftiest lawyers available to get him off on mental incompetence. In a couple of years he'd be out and up to his old tricks again. No, this guy was beyond the law, just like most rich people. He had no remorse for what he'd done, didn't give a shit for the women he'd killed or the people's lives he'd shattered.

Sullivan made up his mind then and there. Jerome Faraday Jr. deserved to die.

Shoving the photos back into the folder, Sullivan nodded resolutely. "Very preppy," he grunted under his breath.

"Isn't he, though," Sanson commented. "His Ivy League style is part of his lure. Good-looking, clean-cut, the boy your mother always wanted you to bring home. His victims probably melted for him. Then, when he got them alone, he showed them how he really felt about women."

"I think I have all I need," Sullivan said, sliding out of the booth. "You won't be hearing from me for a while."

Sanson nodded. "Just don't get your ass blown off down there. I'm counting on you for that Beirut mission we talked about."

"How soon will it be coming down?"

"Nothing is definite yet. We're putting together the commando unit right now. The best men in the military. You'll run the show, of course, and this time you'll have complete amnesty. You do whatever you have to, whichever way you can. The government will be right behind you on this."

"It's time someone beat those terrorists at their own game. They've got it coming, and I'd like to make sure they get it with interest."

"By the time you get back from Mexico, we should have your unit assembled and ready for training."

"Great. See you soon, I hope." Sullivan turned to go, but Sanson called him back.

"Uh, concerning Faraday. Off the record, Jack, give him one for me."

Sullivan nodded grimly. "Count on it."

5

Quintana Roo

The flight in from Mexico City was a flying version of a chaotic Mexican chicken bus minus the chickens—mechanics returning with spare parts, fat women and their kids visiting relatives, a couple of young West German backpackers, a group of uniformed soldiers on leave—and Sullivan had been grateful for that. It was common knowledge that the airline he'd chosen didn't run the tightest fleet in the skies. They seldom bothered to use metal detectors on the stowed luggage for domestic flights because everybody had pots, pans, carburetors, valves, wrenches, tin ducts, all kinds of things in their beat-up bags and strapped valises. That made it easy for Sullivan to transport his latest purchases in his duffel.

The black-market arms dealers in Mexico City weren't nearly as well-stocked as their counterparts in Macao or Vienna, he'd found, but Sullivan still managed to get what he wanted. An M79 grenade launcher and a fresh .44 Auto-Mag pistol. He'd also picked up something new that would be very useful in the jungle, a Heckler & Koch Close Assault Weapons System—CAWS.

The CAWS was a twelve-gauge, bullpup-layout machine shotgun. It was compact and lightweight with the best characteristics of a traditional pump shotgun and

an automatic assault rifle. A semiautomatic, the CAWS
held a detachable, reloadable ten-round box magazine
loaded with single-fléchette cartridges capable of pene-
trating a hard target at ranges up to 150 yards. It
would come in handy for picking off a target at long
range, a definite possibility just in case he couldn't get
close to Faraday. At close range, the CAWS could tear
a man in half. Testing it out in Mexico City, Sullivan
had been very impressed with its straight-line stock,
plastic shroud, high-tech look. More important, the
weapon did everything it promised, with very little re-
coil. He looked forward to putting it to the test in the
field.

Now and then Sullivan would glance at the olive-
drab Cordura duffel bouncing in the compartment behind him as he drove over the rutted dirt road that ran
through the jungle to the isolated village of Santa Celesta, the closest outpost to Faraday's mountain *castillo*.

After landing at Ciudad Chetumal, the capital of the
state of Quintana Roo, near the border of Belize—the
country formerly known as British Honduras—Sullivan
rented a Jeep and headed directly into the Yucatán.
The roads were worse than he expected, so what looked
like eighty-five miles northwest on the map turned out
to be a grueling three and a half hours overland through
heavy tropical jungle. It didn't take long before his
lungs were full of dust, his clothes were sopping with
sweat, and his ass was sore from the nonstop pounding
over rough terrain.

When Sullivan finally arrived in Santa Celesta, it was
siesta time, and only the goats and chickens were up
and around. It gave him a good opportunity to scout
out the town without anyone watching him. He pulled
up in front of the local cantina and cut the engine. The
dead silence buzzed in his ears as he got out of the Jeep
and stretched his legs. It didn't take more than a glance
to tell that the fly-ridden little hole in the middle of the
jungle was not one of the gems of the Yucatán Peninsula.

The streets were uniformly dusty, and no doubt ankle-deep with mud in the rainy season. There was a combination general store and cantina, a one-pump gas station, a telegraph office, and a small stucco church. The rest of the village was made up of corrugated tin shanties. Wiping the sweat from his brow, Sullivan was suddenly uneasy. The quiet seemed unnatural and contrived. The tropical heat was brutal but intoxicating; the jungle seemed too close, as if it threatened to pull him in if he turned his back on it. Santa Celesta reminded Sullivan a little too much of Vietnam, and it wasn't a welcome reminder.

"*Señor.*"

Sullivan turned toward the hoarse whisper coming from behind him.

"*Señor,* over here."

A head peered from the doorway of a small wooden structure set by the side of the road. At first Sullivan thought it was an outhouse, but when the door swung open, he saw that it was a roadside stand selling beer and Coke.

"Nice cold beer here, *señor.* Want one?" The little man held out a can of Tecate in his sun-browned hand, a hard offer to refuse in the tropical heat.

Sullivan walked over to the stand, accepted the beer, popped the top, and downed half the can in one shot. "What do I owe you?" he asked, wondering how much English the vendor really knew.

"Whatever it's worth to you, *señor* Yankee." The little man chuckled, showing how many of his yellow teeth were missing.

"How'd you know I was American?" Sullivan asked.

"You know what they say, 'Only crazy American gringos go out in the midday sun.'" He doubled over, laughing at his own joke.

"You see many Americans down here?"

"Sure. We got our own American millionaire right here in our jungle. Many Americans come and go, his workers, you know? They come to Santa Celesta and they buy beer from Ramón." He patted his chest proudly.

"Pleased to meet you, Ramón." Sullivan extended his huge pawlike hand. If he played his cards right, he might be able to get some information out of this Ramón. "I heard about this rich American, Ramón. That's why I'm here . . . You couldn't tell me how to get there, could you?"

"Sure, I can tell you how to get to Señor Faraday's *castillo.*" Ramón pointed up the dirt road that led out of town. "You take that road for about ten miles, then look for a sign that says . . ."

Listening carefully to Ramón's directions, Sullivan didn't notice the three *federales* who'd just stepped out of the cantina. Their uniforms were dirty and two of them wore crushed peaked caps. They were dark and scruffy-looking, not unlike the stray mongrels that wander the roads all over Mexico. The hatless one had a full black beard; the other two both wore thick mustaches and had a three-day growth of beard on their cheeks. They all wore identical automatic pistols in their belt holsters—9mm Beretta 92SB's.

They eyed Sullivan's Jeep suspiciously. When they overheard Ramón say "Faraday," six bushy eyebrows raised in unison. The hatless *federal* looked at his two companions and nodded slowly, once.

"Thanks for the info, Ramón," Sullivan said, starting to turn back toward the Jeep. Then he suddenly noticed something different in Ramón's expression. There was warning in his eyes.

"Señor," Ramon said, "how about one for the road, eh? You may need something, my friend. That will surely be a rough stretch for you."

Sullivan turned slowly and followed Ramón's glance to the three *federales* glaring at him from the porch of the cantina. In the blink of an eye, he sized up the situation. Their Berettas were pretty fancy weapons for backwater lawmen. Chances were excellent that the guns were gifts from old man Faraday.

They were closer to the Jeep than he was. Sullivan had a remote chance of making a run for it.

He had the Auto-Mag holstered under his bush jacket, but the damn thing was awkward on the draw. They'd probably draw and plug him before he could get a shot off.

Then there was always the possibility that they weren't working for Faraday at all, and unless he was sure, Sullivan didn't want to kill cops.

He walked back toward his Jeep, not too slow, not too fast. The *federales* glared at him without blinking. Everyone seemed to be waiting for someone else to make the first offensive move. Sullivan stared them down, neither yielding nor provoking. He reached the Jeep, climbed in, hit the ignition, and shoved it into reverse.

"Thanks for the big welcome," he grunted under his breath as he moved the stick into first and started up the dirt road toward Faraday's fortress.

As he rammed the Jeep into second, he glanced into the rearview mirror mounted on the fender. The three *federales* were getting into their own vehicle, a battered Toyota four-wheel-drive Land Cruiser. He heard their engine roar to life as the Cruiser lurched forward, following him up the road.

Sullivan continued at his own pace. He would wait and let them make the first move. It was entirely possible that they were just naturally suspicious of strangers and wanted to see what the gringo was up to.

But as Sullivan drove up the rutted road, the jungle grew thicker again, and he had to struggle to keep his mind on the three *federales* following him. His thoughts strayed to another place, another time. The emerald green of sunlight filtered through the jungle vegetation, the huge waving fronds of elephant-ear palms, the insidious tangle of vines, the cloying humidity, the mocking chatter of hidden monkeys—it all reminded him of Nam. And that wasn't good.

Thoughts of Nam triggered a smoldering inner rage that time couldn't extinguish. He had become a killing machine in Nam, and he could feel the Yucatán jungle

turning him into that same almost uncontrollable killing machine. Since the war, he'd always been able to
follow his instincts, keep a low profile, kill when
the time called for it. Sure, there were times when
injustice gnawed at him so bad he turned into that
uncontrollable instrument of vengeance, yet that was
different, that was all for the good. But when he couldn't
put a lid on it, when he performed as he had in the last
days of Nam, the whole world was a free-fire zone for
the Specialist.

The drone of the Land Cruiser climbing the hill
behind him pulled him out of his meandering thoughts.
They were about four miles from the center of Santa
Celesta now, and it was clear that they weren't going to
let him out of their sight. He couldn't let them follow
him all the way up to Faraday's place, though. They'd
see what he was up to. He had to get rid of them.

Outrunning them was impossible; the road was bad
and narrow. There was no place to lose them, and
chances of busting an axle were pretty good. No, he
couldn't tip his hand now. He had to let them catch up
with him, force them to take the next step. He'd figure
out what to do when the moment came. Sullivan always
worked best under pressure.

He downshifted to slow down and let them catch up. It
didn't take long for them to make their move. The
Land Cruiser raced up to Sullivan's tail, horn blaring,
the *federales* shouting at him in Spanish. They motioned
for him to pull over, and when he didn't do it fast
enough to suit them, they pulled up to Sullivan's side
and sideswiped him to force him over.

He slid the Jeep to a halt, then quickly unzipped his
duffel halfway. Just in case he needed more firepower.

The *federales* piled out of their Land Cruiser, and
Sullivan watched closely to see if any Berettas had been
drawn. Surprisingly, they were all still holstered.

The hatless one, the leader, rushed up to Sullivan
and pulled him out of the driver's seat by the bush
jacket. Sullivan could have snapped his arm off at the

shoulder if he chose to, but instead he decided to keep his cool. He was still uncertain as to whether they were corrupt or not. They could simply be trying to throw a scare into him and run him out of the area. It was a police rule of thumb around the world: No strangers, no trouble. Their behavior could simply be a means of eliminating trouble.

The other two *federales* hauled Sullivan up by the arms while their leader frisked him. When the bearded *federal* pulled the Auto-Mag out of Sullivan's shoulder holster, his tiny eyes bulged. He held the long-barreled automatic pistol as if it were a sacred pre-Columbian icon. Obviously they'd never seen a weapon as unusual as the Auto-Mag, and it seemed to inspire a kind of macho awe in them not unlike the devotion the ancient Aztec Indians had for Quetzalcoatl, the great feathered serpent and god of learning. It was just the kind of distraction Sullivan needed.

These boys had never had to deal with karate maneuvers, so they had no defense against the Specialist as he snapped his arms free, knocking the wind out of the flunkies with punishing elbow thrusts, and hammering the leader with his own head.

The leader dropped the Auto-Mag and clutched the bloody splat that used to be his nose. Sullivan scooped up his gun and quickly reholstered it while one of the flunkies to his side reached for his pistol. Sullivan automatically lunged at the man's throat with a spear-hand *nukite*, then followed with a lightning *yoko-geri*, a side kick that sent the *federal* flying to the ground, smashing his head against a wheel rim of the Land Cruiser and knocking him out cold.

The other flunky grabbed Sullivan from behind, but a quick side flip forced the man to the ground. He scrambled back up and went for his gun, but before it cleared the holster, Sullivan's roundhouse kick to the man's temple brought on instantaneous unconsciousness.

Staring at his two amigos out cold, the leader was paralyzed with fear when Sullivan whipped around to face him. In his fear, he forgot that he had a gun. He just stood in fright, waiting for the worst to happen.

Sullivan could have done his worst, but he took pity on the poor bloodied bastard. A mercifully quick *shuto* knife-hand to a precise spot behind the man's ear sent him to dreamland too.

He dragged the unconscious *federales* to their Land Cruiser and propped them up in the seats. Passersby would think they'd just pulled over to the side of the road to take their siesta. Lifting the hood of the Cruiser, he yanked the distributor cap from the engine, swung it by the wires like a bull-roarer, and flung in far into the jungle. Just in case they decided to go looking for him after they came to.

Sullivan then inspected the damage to his Jeep. No great harm done, he thought as he pulled the crushed fender away from the wheel with his bare hands.

He jumped in and started the engine. It was time to get going. He had work to do.

According to Ramón, there should be a sign a few miles up this road. Just beyond the signpost, he had said, there'd be a narrow path off to the left that ran right through the jungle. Ramón had told him it would be overgrown with ferns and vines, and nearly impossible to find. But if he found that path and followed it in about two or three miles he'd find Faraday's *castillo* at the end.

Sullivan bounced along the dirt road for a couple of miles until he came to the rotting signpost whose paint had peeled off long ago. Its useless condition meant that few travelers came out this way anymore. Perfect place for a psycho killer to hide out.

Downshifting into first, Sullivan crawled on, looking for the path Ramón had told him about. He found it about forty yards up ahead; without the tire-tread marks on the dirt road, he would never have seen it. Rubber-plant leaves and hanging moss shaded the trail, making it indistinguishable from the rest of the jungle. As Sullivan knew from his experience in Vietnam, you could cut a trail through the jungle on Monday and by Tuesday afternoon the insidious vegetation would have reclaimed it.

Following the tracks in the road, Sullivan nosed the Jeep into the jungle. Hanging vines and palm fronds brushed his head as he inched forward. After a few yards he stopped and reached back to his duffel. He pulled out a Gurkha kukri, twelve inches of high-carbon, razor-sharp steel. The boomerang-shaped knife was standard issue for the Gurkha mercenaries of Nepal. Sullivan preferred the kukri to a machete. It was just as effective for cutting through the jungle, but was weighted better for hand-to-hand combat. He unsheathed the shiny blade and laid it on the seat next to him. In a tropical jungle there was always a good chance that some slithery bastard would drop down for a bite.

Sullivan put the Jeep in gear and pulled out. Ten mph was about as fast as he could go here. As long as he didn't have to contend with any snakes, the only thing he had to worry about was meeting someone coming down the path from the other direction. He still had a few preparations to make before he made his presence known.

The jungle humidity was overbearing and the mosquitoes were man-eaters. Hypnotized by the drone of the engine, enveloped in emerald-green foliage, Sullivan drifted back to his days in Nam. He had that old feeling again, that gut-wrenching uncertainty that something could come down at any minute, fly out of nowhere right into your face. He started to think about that mission he'd led deep into North Vietnamese territory, to that munitions depot near the Laotian border. The time he nearly bought it. . . .

He was suddenly jolted from his ruminations by the sight of something hideous looming through the trees. The large fragmented shape began to take form in his mind—huge granite blocks, Gothic turrets, crenellated battlements. This had to be the place, Faraday's *castillo*.

Sullivan studied the old Spanish castle. It was like an

ancient monster, a dragon sitting on a stone cliff, bask-
ing in the sun. The path led to a clearing about fifty
yards ahead where a steep ashphalt-paved road curved
up to massive wrought-iron front gates. From what he
could make out, the cliff dropped off sharply behind
the castle, maybe a hundred yards or so straight down
into the jungle. The reports Sanson had given him
deemed the place impregnable; Sullivan could see why
they thought so. But of course "impregnable" wasn't in
the Specialist's vocabulary.

Sullivan reached back to his duffel and pulled out a
coil of nylon rope and a plastic squeeze bottle full of a
clear liquid. Stepping out of the Jeep, he looked around
for an appropriate tree, one with a horizontal branch
just high enough to be out of sight. He found a suitable
candidate about twenty feet off the path, and immediately he tossed the rope over the branch. He tied one
end of the rope to the handles of the duffel, then
doused the entire bag with the liquid animal repellent.
Working quickly, he covered the duffel with palm
branches and then hauled it up, lashing the rope to the
trunk, which he marked with two vertical slashes in the
smooth olive-colored bark. After draping the taut rope
with more branches, Sullivan was satisfied that his arsenal was safely stashed. His plan didn't call for the heavy
artillery just yet. But as every good merc knows, it's
always smart to have a little backup hidden somewhere.

Going back to the Jeep, he sheathed the kukri and
belted it around his waist. He got behind the wheel, felt
for the Auto-Mag under his jacket, and hit the ignition.
Five minutes later he was in the clearing, heading for
the paved road that led up to Faraday's castle.

He gritted his molars as he ground gears to get up
the steep incline. Just be cool, he reminded himself.
Just be cool and don't show off.

The whine of the Jeep's engine alerted a guard
standing watch on the battlements of the castle. Sullivan saw him lift something to his mouth, no doubt a

walkie-talkie, which meant that the welcoming party would be right down.

Sullivan pulled up to the front gate, shut off the engine, and honked the horn a few times as if he were picking up his date. While he waited, he propped one foot up on the dashboard and lit a Lucky Strike.

He hadn't taken three drags off his cigarette when a spiky-haired blond punk no more than twenty years old suddenly came up from behind and jabbed the muzzle on an M16 into the base of Sullivan's skull.

"Put them hands up and git your ass outta there," the punk yelled with a Southern drawl. "Real slow."

Sullivan left his cigarette in his mouth, put up his hands, and slowly got out. He almost laughed out loud when he got a look at the skinny kid menacing him with the big gun. He reminded Sullivan of all those wimpy ARVN infantrymen back in Nam who couldn't even manage to successfully shoot themselves in the foot.

"Okay, pal, be cool. See, I'm cooperating," Sullivan said, staring the kid directly in the eye to distract him.

A lightning kick and the M16 flew out of the kid's hands. A knife-hand strike to the collarbone and the punk was eating dirt.

That's one, Sullivan thought as two more thugs showed up—a burly black guy and a tall lanky white guy. The white guy stuck a revolver in Sullivan's kidneys as the black guy took aim at his gut with a length of pipe, like a home-run slugger at the plate. The slugger started his swing, Sullivan dropped to the ground. The pipe smashed the white guy's forearm so hard he dropped his gun. Then, balancing on his fingertips, Sullivan drove his boot into the slugger's gut.

Two and three, he thought with a smirk. This was textbook karate, no challenge at all.

A fat thug rushed up to him brandishing what at a glance looked like a Simonov SKS-46 assault carbine. Sullivan sneered at the jiggling mountain of running flesh, waiting for him to get closer, closer . . . A forearm block sent the muzzle off to the side, a groin kick sent Fatso to his knees.

Four, that ought to be enough, he decided. Got to look good, but not too good.

The thugs had regrouped by then, and they were all over Sullivan now. Sullivan put up a fight, throwing a few perfunctory knife-hand chops and midsection kicks—even a *keiko*, the chicken-beak finger thrust, into the fat thug's eye socket. After a few minutes, he decided to back off before they started using firearms. He tensed his stomach and took a punch in the gut, then doubled over and pretended to be hurt. They grabbed his arms, and he let them slap a set of handcuffs on him. The slugger and the lanky lumberjack-type hauled him up as Fatso shouted orders.

"Open the gates. Hurry up," Fatso huffed. "K.C., get the hell back on the wall."

The medieval iron gates rose with the drone of an electric motor, and the thugs dragged Sullivan in. Sullivan breathed heavily to make it look like he was exhausted. He hoped his performance was convincing.

6
Like Son, Like Father

Jerome Faraday Sr. sat behind the huge carved rose-
wood desk in his office overlooking the jungle and
gazed through half-glasses at the passport his men had
taken from Sullivan when they frisked him. The
Auto-Mag and the kukri sat side by side on his desk
next to the solid gold double pen holder. He inspected
the passport without emotion, like a man who isn't
particularly hungry reading a menu.

Still handcuffed, Sullivan stood before the elderly
billionaire, flanked by the slugger and the lumberjack.
Fatso stood off to the side with a .357 Magnum drawn
and ready.

Sullivan studied Faraday—his immaculate white silk
suit, the hanging chicken neck, the liver-spotted hands,
the perfectly manicured nails. Based on the pictures of
Jerome Junior he'd seen, Sullivan noticed the strong
family resemblance. They both had the same greyhound-
slender build, violet-blue eyes, straight patrician nose,
and identical flat thin-lipped mouth. Besides the obvious age difference, the only thing that Faraday Junior
had that his father didn't was a full head of hair.

Faraday Senior let out a long sigh as he flipped a
page of the passport. "Stark . . . Richard Stark . . ." he
murmured to himself. Then he looked up over his

glasses and stared at Sullivan. "I assume this isn't your real name, Mr. Stark."

"You can assume whatever you want," Sullivan replied coolly.

Faraday continued to stare at him, letting the silence stretch out uncomfortably long. Sullivan stared back without blinking.

"Who are you working for, sir? The IRS, the CIA, FBI, one of my competitors, who? Which of my many crimes are you here to redress, Mr. Stark? Tax evasion? Corporate theft? What? Or is simply being very successful my greatest sin? Are you some egalitarian angel here to punish me for being rich? Speak up."

"As I've already said, my name is Stark and I'm a mercenary. I heard you were hiring, and I came for a job." Sullivan cast a loathing glance at Fatso. "And from the looks of things, you need me."

The fat man took a step toward Sullivan. "You fuckin'—"

"Quiet," Faraday barked, cross as an old schoolmarm. Fatso obeyed like a dog.

"Do you really expect me to believe that you're simply a soldier of fortune looking for employment?"

Sullivan exhaled a little laugh. "If I was here to kill you, why did I come up to the front gate? Wouldn't I have tried to sneak in to make the hit?"

"Perhaps. But maybe this is the ploy you've devised to get into my fortress. Men of your ilk are known to be stupidly daring. You tend to go in balls-first, as it were."

"You're going to believe what you want to believe," Sullivan tossed back. "My name's Stark and I'm here for a job. Now, do you want me or not?" Faraday was no fool. He knew Sullivan's method was probably the easiest way to get into the *castillo*. The only way Sullivan was going to pull the mission off was to convince Faraday Senior here and now that he was just a merc looking for a gig. "Do I have the job or what?" Sullivan repeated.

Faraday didn't answer. Instead he picked up the

Auto-Mag and turned it in his hand, examining the weapon the way a connoisseur checks the color of a fine wine. "This is quite a weapon, sir. Not your standard CIA issue. More like the kind of gun a trained killer would use, a man who relishes a good kill."

Sullivan forced a sick smile to make the old man think he agreed.

"All right, Mr. Stark—or whatever your name is— you've got the job. I was going to have you tortured to find out who sent you, but I have a feeling you're a bona fide mercenary. I like to trust my feelings now and then, Mr. Stark." Faraday set down the gun and gazed out the window at the endless jungle. "My feelings aren't always on the money, though. Once, a long time ago, a man named Williams came to me with some very good manufacturing ideas and a fistful of patents he'd acquired. He knew a lot about metal alloys and he'd devised a program for making cheaper auto parts out of cheaper metals. I liked Williams. He appreciated money, and he had the drive to go out and make it. I felt good about him and I made him my partner in a manufacturing venture."

Faraday swiveled around in his chair and faced Sullivan again. "But I was all wrong about Williams. He wasn't satisfied with the deal he had with me. I found out that he was talking to my competitors, testing the waters as it were, trying to find a better nest for himself. Now, that made me angry. Disloyalty is unacceptable in my empire, Mr. Stark. It weakens the power base and makes us vulnerable. It's the enemy within."

Faraday reached down to the bottom drawer of his desk and came up with a human skull. "Meet Mr. Williams, Mr. Stark," he said, placing the skull on his blotter facing Sullivan. "I taught him a one-time lesson in loyalty. After I confronted him with his betrayal, I had the immense satisfaction of personally pushing him into a vat of acid at our plant. I keep him as a reminder to myself. A reminder of what I must do to those who betray me and the Faraday name. Many men have been

disloyal to Faraday International and they have all met
Mr. Williams in the hereafter. Do you see what I'm
saying, Mr. Stark?"

Sullivan saw perfectly. Faraday Senior was also a
murderer, many times over. He deserved to die. Like
father, like son.

"For your sake, Mr. Stark, I hope you aren't lying to
me," Faraday said. "Take those handcuffs off him," he
ordered the fat man. "Get him a rifle and put him on
duty immediately. Sentry duty is a good place for a new
employee. If you do well up on the battlements, you
can move up to more challenging work."

The fat man unlocked the cuffs and the other two
goons started to lead him out.

"Hey, hold on," Sullivan objected, pulling away from
their grip. "What about my stuff?" He pointed to the
Auto-Mag and the kukri on the desk.

"You may have your knife back, but the pistol is
mine. Let's just consider it my finder's fee for getting
you the job."

"What are you talking about? I found *you*."

"No matter," Faraday said. "This is too fine a weapon
for the likes of you. Besides, up on the wall you'll need
an automatic rifle, not this." Faraday picked up the
Auto-Mag and the skull and deposited them both in his
bottom drawer.

"Welcome to the company, Mr. Stark." Faraday forced
a sarcastic smile. "Now, get to work."

Sullivan grumbled a curse under his breath as the
thugs ushered him out of Faraday's office. Jerome Faraday Sr. had a lot to learn about mercs. You don't take
food away from a Doberman, and you don't take a gun
away from a merc. When the time came, Jerome Senior
would learn this lesson.

"Okay, Stark, this is your post," said Ludlow, the fat
man. "You stay up here on the wall and you watch the
road and the clearing. If you spot anything, get on the

walkie-talkie pronto. Now, that isn't too hard for you, is it?"

"I'll manage," Sullivan said distractedly as he examined the Armalite 15 assault rifle he'd just been given. The AR15 was a decent light weapon, sometimes used by SWAT teams, but this one needed work. Sullivan couldn't afford to have his only gun misfire or jam on him.

The air was almost as heavy and humid up on the wall as it was down in the jungle, and he had no cover from the relentless sun. This was without a doubt the shit detail for the incompetents, Sullivan thought, noting that the only other sentry on the wall was that spike-headed punk fuck-up he'd disarmed so easily at the front gate.

"Hey, Stark, you listening to me?" Ludlow shouted.

Sullivan wasn't listening. Ludlow had been yammering ever since they left Faraday's office, trying to intimidate Sullivan with his boasts of how many men, women, and children he'd slaughtered in his long career as a hired killer. Shutting the fat man out, Sullivan was now preoccupied with taking in the layout of the *castillo*, memorizing where all the sentries were, trying to figure out where Jerome Faraday Jr. was.

"I'm talking to you, Stark!" the fat man yelled in his ear.

"Eat shit, Fats," Sullivan growled.

Ludlow's face turned red with fury as he grabbed Sullivan by the front of his bush jacket. "Hey, fuck-face, I told you never to call me that!"

Sullivan paused and looked at the fat fist as if it were a stain on his jacket. Ludlow drew the commando knife from his belt sheath and was about to ram it into Sullivan's side when the Specialist went into action.

Sullivan grabbed the fat man's wrist and smashed the forearm over his knee repeatedly, as if he were breaking a stick. When the blade clattered on the stone walkway, Sullivan put Ludlow in an armlock, twisted the tub of lard around, whipped out the kukri, and nestled the man's Adam's apple in a crook of cold steel. "How'd you like to lose twenty ugly pounds real quick, Fats?"

Ludlow didn't dare answer for fear the movement of his vocal cords would cause the blade to cut flesh.

"Now, you listen to me, Fats. Do not—I repeat, *do not* fuck with me. I'm dying to slit you down the middle, from your fat throat to your itty-bitty balls, just to watch your guts spill out like a butchered hog, and I won't need much provocation to do it. Now, I know you're saying to yourself that this asshole is just blowing air, that you'll get me for this. Well, you're wrong, Fats. I don't bluff. And just so you remember that, I'll write you a memo."

Sullivan scraped Ludlow's beard under his chin with the razor-sharp kukri. Hair, skin, and blood collected on the blade as Sullivan plowed a strip through the fat man's mangy beard. Ludlow gritted his teeth as the pain seared through his jowls. When Sullivan finally let him go, he clutched his throat and ran for the infirmary, growling, "I'll get you, you bastard, I'll get you," as he waddled off.

The punk strolled across the battlement, applauding Sullivan as he approached. "Way to go, man. Ludlow had it comin'." There was a joint dangling from his mouth.

Sullivan eyeballed him suspiciously. The punk could still be holding a grudge for what happened at the front gate.

The punk came up to Sullivan, and instead of offering a handshake, he offered Sullivan a toke off his joint.

Sullivan shook his head, the bloody kukri still in his hand, silently waiting for the punk to make a move.

"Hey, listen, man, no hard feelings about you knocking me down out front. It's sorta nice to see a real pro in action for a change."

"I thought all you guys were pros here," Sullivan said.

"Are you kidding? Man, this outfit is somewhere

between F Troop and McHale's Navy. Bush-leaguers."
The punk stopped to take another long drag on his
joint. "By the way, the name's K.C."

The kid seemed friendly enough; Sullivan decided to
let him talk to see what kind of information he'd spill.

Sullivan nodded and smiled grimly. "If everyone hates
Ludlow's guts, why hasn't anyone put him in his place
before this?"

"Some of the guys get along with him just fine. Jake
and Reece, the other guys who brought you down, are
his main men. But there are about ten of us who
wouldn't cry too hard if a python swallowed the three
of them whole."

Division in the ranks. That could help when the time
comes, Sullivan thought.

"How'd you end up here?" Sullivan asked casually.
"You don't seem like the kind of guy who usually takes
this kind of work."

"Very observant, Stark. I hate this fuckin' gig, man,
but unfortunately, I'm a very popular guy with the
federal narcs, and they'd just love to get their hands on
me. See, at one time I had a very sweet piece of the pie
in Palm Beach. A very select clientele of rich folks.
When they needed coke, smack, smoke, anything, they
just gave ole K.C. a call and put in their order. I was
livin' high, man. You can't imagine how nice I had it."

"What happened?"

"This rich bitch OD'ed on some smack I sold her.
Her lover, this ugly dyke, got crazy and threatened to
turn me in, so I did what I had to do. A slug in the
brain took care of her, or at least that's what I thought.
See, the maid was hiding in the closet pissin' her panties, and she witnessed the whole thing. After I left, she
called the cops. The fuckers almost got me."

"How'd you get away from them?"

"Mr. Faraday smuggled me out. He was my best
customer. Always bought a lot of shit just to have around
the house for his guests. I begged him for help, and he
smuggled me down here. The bastard told me he had a

good job for me down here. He didn't tell me it was standing on this fucking wall watching a lot of green nothing."

A drug dealer and a murderer. Sullivan wouldn't have any problem putting K.C. out when the time came. He deserved it for all the misery his "product" must have caused and all the slime who profited from his trade.

"I heard Faraday is hiding someone out down here. That's why he needs all the firepower. Must be somebody pretty important." Sullivan was playing dumb to see what he could find out about Jerome Junior.

"Faraday's kid, that's who we're protecting here. But as far as being important . . . well, I guess he's pretty important to his old man for some reason." K.C. sucked greedily on the roach of his joint until he burned his fingers.

"I'm not reading you, K.C. Is he or isn't he important?"

K.C. lowered his voice. "You didn't hear it from me, but the rumor is that Junior likes to kill chicks. Very kinky and all that. That's only rumor, though, because I've never actually seen Junior. None of us has."

"How come?"

"Faraday keeps him locked up on the second floor. As a matter of fact, I don't even have clearance to be on the second floor."

K.C. pointed to the rear section of the fortress, the side that overlooked the sheer rock drop and the endless expanse of jungle below. It made sense that Faraday Junior was being kept there; from the outside it was the most inaccessible part of the *castillo*.

"The only people allowed on the second floor are Ludlow, Reece, Jake, and the maids. But the *señoritas* don't stick around very long, and they're always locals who only speak Spanish, so I never get any info out of them. Oh, yeah, I almost forgot about Peter. Big mother, at least six-ten, and a crazy Rasta from Jamaica to boot, with dreadlocks out to here." K.C. extended his arms over his head. "That ole boy looks like he's got a dead octopus on his head. But you won't catch me messin' with him. Nossir. I know for a fact that he slaughtered a whole task force of FBI narcs in Miami last year. Offed four fuckin' feds all by himself." The punk's drugged-out expression turned deadly serious when he talked about Peter the Rasta.

"All I know about Junior is what I hear," K.C. continued, rubbing his cocaine-corroded nose furiously. "Every now and then you hear some bimbo screaming her lungs out. Junior getting his jollies, I guess."

As if on cue, a terrified scream cut through the midday heat like an air-raid siren. Sullivan stared down at the leaded windows of the second-floor hall, angrily clenching the AR15 until he was white-knuckled.

"See what I mean?" K.C. chuckled.

A deep frown creased Jerome Faraday Sr.'s face when he opened the door to his son's suite and saw what was going on. Teresa, the middle-aged matronly maid, was tied to a chair with torn strips of bedding. Her blouse had been ripped open, and her abundant breasts were exposed. Jerome Junior, neatly dressed in a pink Izod polo shirt and crisp khaki pants, was holding a large flaming candle over her, dripping hot wax onto her nipples.

"Jerome! Jerome, stop that!" Faraday Senior ordered.

Faraday Junior's eyes were glazed and a perverse half-smile was plastered across his face. He was lost in a sadistic trance.

"Dammit, Jerome, do you know how hard it is to get reliable servants in this benighted country?"

Faraday Senior rushed up to his crazed son and wrestled the candle from his hand. Enraged by the interference, Jerome Junior glared at his father, a twisted grimace across his face. "I'm not through! Give me the candle."

When his father didn't comply immediately, Jerome struck him hard with the back of his hand, then started to pummel him with his balled fists. Faraday doubled over, trying to shield his head.

Breathing hard, Faraday fought his way back up from his crouch, reached into his breast pocket, then grabbed one of Jerome's wrists. Throwing him off balance, Faraday brought down the blackjack he always carried, smashing his son behind the ear and knocking him out cold. Jerome slumped back onto the bed.

"Jerome, Jerome," he clucked, "what am I to do with you, Jerome? You're thirty-seven years old and I have to treat you like an infant. Do you think I like keeping you locked up in here as if it were a prison?"

He started to untie Teresa's bindings, and as soon as she was free, she bolted from the room. "I suppose that's the last we'll be seeing of you," he muttered.

In a few minutes, Jerome came to, rubbing his head gingerly. "Why did you have to hit me again, Father? It's not fair. You treat me like an animal."

"I treat you like an animal because you act like an animal. You're a disgrace to the family name, Jerome. If I hadn't come to your rescue, you would have been a scandal-sheet oddity. I can just imagine how the press would have dragged our name through the mud. You're indiscreet, Jerome. A Faraday can do anything he likes in privacy, but in public a Faraday's reputation must be impeccable. I warned you to keep your little pleasures a secret, but you let it get out of hand."

Jerome turned away and didn't answer. He couldn't care less about the Faraday name. He just wanted to be free so he could do what the voices in his head told him he needed to do.

"Don't pout now, Jerome. I'll get you a whore tonight and you can do with her as you like. You have my word."

Faraday Senior turned to leave, stopping once to grumble over his stained white pants.

Jerome scowled at his father and gave him the finger behind his back. The carved mahogany door slammed shut, and Jerome once again heard what was becoming a familiar refrain, the sounds of a procession of dead bolts locking him in.

7
O What a Tangled Web

As the brilliant orange sun set over the jungle, Sullivan stood on the veranda outside the mess hall, once again lost in thought. His mind never left his mission; executing Faraday and Son was all-important to him. Still, the jungle outside nagged at him like something elusive dancing in his peripheral vision. Despite the unmistakable aromas of Mexican cooking, the kitchen help chattering away in Spanish, and the faraway strains of a servant's guitar strumming, the Yucatán jungle was too damn similar to the jungles of Nam.

Memories of that last Long-Range Reconnaissance Patrol came back to him. Sullivan and his whole platoon nearly bought it for good that time. Their objective was to destroy a munitions depot near the Cambodian border deep inside North Vietnamese territory. It had started out like any other lurps mission—suicidal. That was normal for a Sullivan operation. His reputation as the Specialist always instilled confidence in the men he led, but something was different that time. And when Sullivan realized what it was, it was almost too late.

He'd had the usual minimal intelligence on this particular munitions depot, but that had never posed a problem before. Lurps had just one basic method—

infiltrate and destroy the target any way you could. And Sullivan was the best. Still, he should have suspected trouble when things started going too smoothly.

Once his team had crossed the DMZ into the North, they encountered a small VC patrol. Apparently the dinks were licking their wounds, having sustained heavy injuries in a firefight in the DMZ the day before. When Sullivan's point man sent back word that a badly shot-up enemy patrol was bivouacked up ahead, the men almost laughed out loud. They figured it would be target practice . . . until Sullivan pointed something out to them.

He'd spotted an object behind a stand of palm fronds; a black fifty-gallon steel drum, between the Americans and the enemy. This was no temporary camp, and those VC's weren't hurting. Sullivan saw the situation for what it was. A trap.

The steel drum was filled with stolen U.S.-issue foo gas, a mixture of napalm and liquid explosives. foo gas drums were detonated with blasting caps from wired hand detonators positioned out of harm's way. When the blasting cap went off, the foo gas drum exploded, sending liquid flames in every direction in a fifty-yard radius. Those who survived the foo gas burns and shrapnel would make easy targets for the assault rifles of the VC "wounded." Charlie was insidious; he thought of everything.

Sullivan immediately moved in and cut the blasting-cap wires of the foo gas drum, but where there was one, there were usually a half-dozen and he knew it would take hours of noisy hacking through jungle growth to find the others. A direct attack on the VC was obviously out of the question, because the VC would set off the other drums hidden in the bush. No, there was only one solution. Sullivan had to sneak into the camp himself and take out the VC ringers. But there were complications . . . there were always complications—

"Hey, Stark!" K.C. called out from the doorway. "Chow time. Come on before there ain't no more."

The sun was below the horizon now, and the sky took on an eerie cobalt-blue hue. A tiny full moon marred the empty sky like a bullet hole in a blue satin sheet. Sullivan stared down at the steaming black jungle once more before he turned to go in.

The mess hall had two long rough-wood tables and twenty or so twine-bottomed ladder-back chairs. Guards were seated at both tables, shoveling chicken and re-fried beans into their mouths, cramming it all in with tortillas, which were stacked like pancakes on both ends of each table. As he entered the room, Sullivan took a quick head count. Sixteen of the thugs were there. Sanson's report said Faraday kept a squad of about twenty at the *castillo*. There had to be two guys on duty up on the wall, which left two, maybe three others inside guarding Faraday Junior.

He looked around for the giant Rasta that K.C. had told him about, but he was nowhere to be seen.

Ludlow was sitting at the head of one of the tables, stuffing his face. He'd had to shave his beard off to have his cut dressed, and his naked jowls were a disgusting clam white. He glared as Sullivan took a seat at the next table. When Jake and Reece saw who Ludlow was looking at, they turned in their seats and gave Sullivan the same dead-eye stare.

Sullivan filled his plate, grabbed a bottle of beer, and ate quietly, listening to the conversation around him.

"Hey, Ludlow," a burly guy with a Popeye squint called out, "what's so fuckin' special about this Faraday kid that we got to guard him so close? So he's killed a lot of broads, so what? He's only got us beat in numbers."

The other men laughed raucously.

"Got to admit, there is something to hearing them girls scream their bloody heads off before they go," commented one cutthroat from Louisiana named Burke, who was wearing mirrored sunglasses and a battered Stetson. "Me and some buddies of mine hit up a convent just for the hell of it one night. I hated nuns since I was a kid. They were mean to me in school, and I wanted to get back at them. We found nine of them sisters. Kept them hostage for a couple of days so we could show them what they'd missed by being celibate, then we sent them all to heaven. With bows and arrows." His wet laugh sounded like sizzling bacon on a hot griddle. The whole room broke into hysterical laughter. All except Sullivan.

Sullivan dropped his fork and nudged K.C. "Hey, K.C., where's the can around here?"

"Huh?" The thugs were making so much noise the punk couldn't hear Sullivan.

"I said where's the can? The head, the john." Sullivan raised his voice.

"Ah, *sí!*" the punk chortled. "Montezuma's Revenge strikes again." He said it so that everyone could hear. "Tough luck, Stark. Hang a right out that door. It's down the end of the hall on the left."

The thugs jeered as Sullivan left. All except one. Ludlow just kept staring silently at him, throwing daggers with his deadly gaze.

Sullivan turned down the hall, trying to get his bearings and locate Jerome Junior's room, no easy feat since the *castillo* was originally designed to defy infiltrators, with deliberate dead ends and narrow mazelike hallways. Its layout was complication number one. Number two was the fact that he'd had to leave his rifle back in the mess hall. Carrying the AR15 to the toilet would have looked too suspicious, so all he had was his kukri by his side. Complications, always complications.

Even though no one would miss him for a while, thinking he was stuck on the john, he knew he had to work fast. Ludlow was out to get him, and he'd be the first to suspect something if Sullivan was gone too long.

The hallways were dimly lit with electric wall sconces every twenty-five feet. They dimmed now and then; the generator wasn't working smoothly. There was no carpeting in this wing, but Sullivan was experienced in walking silently on the balls of his feet, moving like a shadow. That's how he had moved through the jungle in Nam as he approached that VC trap base, the one wired to the foo gas drums.

After he had ordered his men to retreat fifty yards in case the dinks heard him and set off the blasting caps, Sullivan had crept through the jungle, circling the camp so that he could spy on them from the rear. He took a position behind the low branches of a tree and watched Charlie for a while. There were four of them, in phony bandages, two of them doing a great job of moaning in pain. They had a fire going, and one tent set up. Sullivan couldn't see any sign of the hand detonators, though. They had to be inside the tent, protected from the regular afternoon monsoon rains that drenched the jungle every day without fail. Sullivan quickly sized up the situation. His plan was viable, except for one thing. Was there someone inside the tent guarding the hand detonators? It was an unknown he'd had to live with.

The VC were passing around a bottle of clear liquor, rice wine, which they stole from their own peasants. They were far from alert, and none of them heard Sullivan crawling on his belly to the back of their tent. Gritting his teeth, Sullivan had pulled out his commando knife, taken a deep breath, and decided to risk it. His first incision into the green canvas was slow and delicate, a two-inch cut worthy of a brain surgeon. He peered in, holding his breath, and then a big grin spread across his face. Eight Russian-made hand detonators sitting on a tarp all by themselves. Sullivan enlarged the slit, crept in, and went to work cutting wires to disarm the foo gas explosives. When he was finished, he tucked into a crouch, cradled his M16 automatic rifle, and silently adjusted it from semi- to full automatic. He pressed his lips together, breathing evenly, then lunged through the flaps of the tent, spitting slugs into the four shocked VC.

"Good-bye, Charlie," he growled as he emptied his clip into the enemy. . . .

It had been a nice clean kill, complete and final. And that's what Sullivan wanted for this mission. But the layout of the *castillo* turned out to be more complex than he'd thought, and he ended up wandering up and down empty hallways for almost ten minutes before he found a sign of Faraday Junior's presence. Peering around yet another corner, he spotted a thug he hadn't seen before. The man was leaning against the banister post of a stairway, a submachine gun carelessly held in one hand, a burning cigarette in the other.

When Sullivan sauntered around the corner, the guard stuck the cigarette in his mouth and whipped the SMG up, pointing it straight at Sullivan.

"Take it easy, pal," Sullivan said casually, holding up his hands. "I'm the new guy. Name's Stark."

"So what?" the thug grumbled.

"Old man Faraday sprang for steaks, baked potatoes, and good whiskey for the guys tonight. Nice change from the usual wetback slop they feed you, I hear." Sullivan smiled amiably. "Ludlow sent me to relieve you so you won't miss out."

The man's face relaxed. Sullivan could see the thought of steak and whiskey soaking into the man's consciousness.

"Best fuckin' steak I ever had," Sullivan said, tempting the man further. "And Johnnie Walker. Better hurry, though. It's going fast. Ludlow says I'm supposed to watch your post until you're through eating."

"Thanks, Stark. You're okay." The guard dropped his gun and patted Sullivan on the shoulder as he turned to go. Then he stopped short and started to turn around. "Hey, wait a minute. You don't have a gun."

When the guard turned all the way around, he glimpsed the cold-steel flash of the kukri in Sullivan's hand. Sullivan grinned humorlessly. "That's okay, pal. I've got this."

Jerome Faraday Sr. sat at his desk toying with a brass scorpion paperweight, considering the man who sat opposite him. He glanced up at the huge portrait that hung on the wall above his visitor's head, as if seeking advice from his stern ancestor. Sumner W. Faraday, the first Faraday to make a million dollars. The family resemblance was remarkable—they all had the same cold blue eyes and the same twisted grins. The only thing that shone in Sumner's dull portrait was the walnut-sized diamond stickpin he wore in his silk cravat. Sumner had made his fortune using slaves to mine diamonds in South Africa. To Jerome Faraday Sr.'s way of thinking, Sumner had been a true genius when it came to personnel management.

Faraday looked back at the dark-haired man who'd just come to him with a proposition. He could smell the man's incredible greed. It was like a dead fish in the room. But of course, everyone who came to see Faraday smelled of greed. The fact that this fellow was just another petty man with a price shouldn't obscure the fact that he might have something worthwhile to offer. Faraday decided to give him a little more line.

"So, Mr. Preminger, you say that my son and I are in mortal danger, that there is someone out there 'gunning' for me, as it were. Is that correct?"

Preminger was a study in classic Manhattan cool. He took his time lighting another cigarette before he answered. "That's right, Mr. Faraday."

"Yes, well, at the risk of seeming naive, why don't you just spell out what you want from me? How much do you want and what exactly will I be getting for the price?" Whatever Preminger's price was, Faraday knew he could pay it easily. It just better be worth the time he was wasting with this fool.

"I'm not an unreasonable man, Mr. Faraday." Preminger smiled slickly. "All I want is twenty grand and I'll tell you who's been sent to get you, including a full description of the man's appearance."

"Man? One man? I'm supposed to worry about one man trying to get into my fortress, past my personal force? What kind of fool do you take me for?" Faraday's cold blue eyes were suddenly red hot.

"This one man is worth the ten best mercenaries money can buy. He's known in the trade as a killing machine. But the unique thing about him is that he can't be stopped or bought off once he's got his mind made up. He's like a nuclear warhead—once he's launched on a mission, there's no calling him back. And I know for a fact that your son is his target."

Faraday wanted to remain skeptical, but the way Preminger described this man, almost with deadly reverence, made him think twice. His instincts told him that he should know about such a man. Twenty thousand dollars was a steal for that kind of information.

"All right, Mr. Preminger, you have a deal." Faraday took out his key ring, unlocked the top-right-hand drawer of his desk, and pulled out his steel-gray petty-cash box. Petty cash for petty men, he liked to say. Licking his thumb, he began to count out bank-issued bundles of bills and lay them down in front of him as if he were playing solitaire.

When he was through, there were twenty bundles of crisp one-hundred-dollar bills making Preminger's greed rise in him like hungry piranha in a slimy pool. Faraday counted the money again, gathered it into one neat pile, and placed the brass scorpion on top of the mound.

"I'm listening, Mr. Preminger."

Preminger's cool had shattered; the sight of so many portraits of Alexander Hamilton drove him to distraction. "Huh? . . . Oh, yeah. Ah, the man's name is Sullivan, Jack Sullivan. But he's also known as the Specialist."

"The Specialist . . ." Faraday mumbled, starting to go pale. Wasn't that the name of the man who killed the Blue Man and destroyed his entire terrorist network? Faraday had been the Blue Man's client, and at the time he was very sorry to hear that his terrorist service was no more. The Blue Man's people were the best when it came to wholesale death and destruction. But if this Specialist could obliterate an entire camp of trained killers, twenty-one mere thugs and murderers would pose little problem for him. Faraday was beginning to be concerned.

"How do you know that this Sullivan fellow is out to get my son?"

"I was there when he took the job."

"You?" Faraday's temper flared. He had half a mind to take that fine pistol he'd taken from the new man and use it on this insect from New York.

"He was hired by some of the relatives of the women your son killed. They hired me first to check him out, make sure he was all he was cracked up to be. He is, believe me. Based on my report to them, they hired him. Vengeance for what he considers a good cause is his thing, Mr. Faraday. He's on a holy mission now . . . as it were." The smirk returned to Preminger's lips.

"Well, what does he look like, dammit!" Faraday yelled impatiently. "How will we know who he is? Describe him."

Preminger calmly reached into the breast pocket of his tan sports jacket and pulled out a photo. He dropped the picture in front of Faraday and scooped up his fee all in one smooth move. The picture was a blowup of Sullivan stalking up to Kiddie-porn King Harry Babcock's old house in the country. It was one of many surveillance shots Preminger had taken of Sullivan that day.

Faraday's pasty white face turned angry red, but his voice remained calm. "We have a fifth column, Mr. Preminger."

"A what?"

"A fifth column, an infiltrator, an enemy within our walls." He threw down the photo, his eyes burning holes into it. "Stark, Richard Stark . . . my new guard."

"He's here?" Preminger was alarmed. If Sullivan saw him here, he was a dead man for sure.

"Now, don't upset yourself, Mr. Preminger. Mr. Sullivan will be dealt with. It's a very basic management technique. I'm sure you've heard of it."

Preminger shook his head. It was his turn to be unnerved by the other man's unnatural calm.

Faraday looked past Preminger to the portrait of Sumner W. Faraday. "Last hired, first fired. Or should I say 'terminated'?"

Sullivan dragged the guard's body to a broom closet under the stairway he'd been watching, leaving a trail of blood from the dead man's hacked throat. Scooping up the Uzi, he quickly checked the clip and released the safety, them mounted the red-carpeted steps two at a time. If the lure of steak and whiskey worked once, Sullivan figured he'd use it on the next guard. Just walk normally up to the next guy and tell him he was being relieved for—

But when he saw the guard standing outside Faraday Junior's suite, Sullivan immediately doubted that anything as conventional as steak and Scotch would appeal to this monster. This had to be Peter the Rasta. Leaning against the wall, the giant black man was higher than the door frame, and his dreadlocks sprung out of his head like grotesque tree branches. His face was as ugly as a mountain gorilla's, and his eyes appeared to glow red from all the marijuana he'd consumed in his life. Right now he was working on a smoldering *spliff* the size of a blackjack. Sullivan noticed that he had an Uzi SMG of his own stuck in his waistband right over his crotch.

The Rasta seemed slow and out of it, but in the middle of a toke he suddenly whipped out his weapon and leveled it on Sullivan. "Who you?" he growled, smoke swirling through his dreadlocks.

"Hey, mellow out, man," Sullivan said. "I'm the new guy. Stark's the name."

"Stop. Put down the gun, mon, or I kill you now." The Rasta sneered, showing rows of perfect yellow teeth.

Sullivan did as he was told, lowering his Uzi to the carpet. As he approached the giant, he couldn't help wincing at the overpowering stench of marijuana and body odor.

"What you want, mon?" Peter demanded, glaring at Sullivan with his beady red eyes.

"K.C. told me you might be in the market for a little *ganja*. It's pretty good shit, and I got a lot to unload."

As soon as Peter heard the Jamaican word for "pot," the gun went slack in his hand and he flashed a hungry gorilla smile at Sullivan.

That's it, my friend, Sullivan thought as he approached. Lower the Uzi just a little bit more . . . Great!

One expertly timed roundhouse kick sent the Rasta's SMG flying out of his hands. The spear-hand thrust to the gut and the hammer-fist uppercut to the groin that followed would have sent any normal monster to the floor, but Peter was so high he was anesthetized to pain.

Grunting like a wild boar, Peter lunged at Sullivan with long-fingered hands like menacing grappling hooks. He tried to get them into Sullivan's eyes, but Sullivan blocked all his attempts with his extensive repertoire of ancient Oriental maneuvers. The frustrated Rasta finally grabbed Sullivan by the shirtfront and whipped him against the stucco wall. Sullivan felt loose plaster sifting down his collar as his head cracked the wall. Peter lunged again, seizing Sullivan by an arm and a leg and tossing him bodily down the hall.

Now Sullivan was mad. He got to his feet and took a few steps backward.

Peter the Rasta laughed at Sullivan, thinking he was retreating. What he didn't realize was that Sullivan was just making running room for himself. He knew he'd need a good running start to execute a *tobi-mae-geri*, the jumping front kick, high enough to knock his opponent down.

The Rasta started to move forward, but Sullivan's 240-pound mass was now in the air, soaring like a guided missile. Sullivan's iron-tense foot smashed the Rasta's breastbone, toppling him over.

That monstrous Gorgon head hit the carpeted floor so hard he was momentarily stunned. Frantically he looked all around, fighting the tangle of his greasy dreadlocks, searching for his weapon. He spotted the SMG Sullivan had brought, on the floor above his head. He reached back, but it was just inches out of reach. Peter the Rasta crawled to get to it.

But Sullivan already had his kukri drawn, and was bringing it down on the man's outstretched hand. . . .

8

Duel With the Devil

Sullivan sheathed his knife and looked down at the giant carcass sprawled on the burgundy-red carpet. The Rasta's severed hand lay by itself above the lifeless head like a giant black tarantula that had just crawled in from the jungle. Sullivan had to give the man credit for fighting on even after he'd lost his hand. Peter the Rasta had made one last valiant attempt to get to the gun, but Sullivan struck like a cobra, driving the point of the kukri between the third and fourth ribs on the left side, ripping through several major arteries. Sullivan had watched the man's life drain away, but he felt no remorse for him. Peter the Rasta was a known killer. A cop killer.

Sullivan snatched up the Uzi and turned to the door. There were three dead-bolt latches as well as the regular key lock. Once he opened the latches, he'd have no trouble kicking the door down. Then there'd be nothing left between Jerome Faraday Jr. and death.

Rage and anticipation gathered in Sullivan's shoulders as he stepped back and kicked the heavy door— once, twice—smashing the frame to splinters. The door swung back and crashed into the wall behind, cracking stucco and making dust. Sullivan scanned the room. It was dimly lit, unnaturally quiet. Unmade double four-poster bed, colorful Mexican weavings on the walls, massive dark-wood table and chairs. Spanish Inquisition style. But where the hell was Faraday?

With the SMG poised before him, Sullivan stepped carefully into the room. The table was strewn with skin magazines, fuck books, South American porno comics. A centerfold had been torn out of one, and an artistic hand had drawn welts, slashes, and scars all over the model's voluptuous body.

A vein in Sullivan's forehead popped as he clenched his jaw in fury. He had to find this guy, had to grind him into nothing before he killed again.

Suddenly Sullivan smelled something, a whiff of cigarette smoke. He spun around on his heel, Uzi leveled for fire, ready to pull the trigger. But the sight of Jerome Faraday Jr. standing on the threshold of the next room surprised Sullivan.

He'd expected some kind of sluglike mutant, a preppy turned into a drooling wacko. It was a natural assumption; he knew the guy was kept locked up night and day by Jerome Senior. But this guy looked like a college kid who'd just crawled out of an all-night beer blast. He looked much younger than his reported age, and the clothes he now wore—a pair of jogging shorts and a polo shirt with wide horizontal stripes—made him seem even younger. His hair was disheveled and his eyes were half-closed, as if he'd just woken up. Standing in that doorway, he looked like someone who could kill only defenseless women.

"Who the hell are you?" Faraday demanded arrogantly. Not waiting for a reply, he stuck the smoldering cigarette in his mouth and stumbled into the room. "Don't tell me. You're another one of Daddy's babysitters." He acted the part of the haughty aristocrat, the kind who treats people like dogshit on his shoe.

"Wrong, Faraday. I don't work for your father. I work for someone else."

"Oh, really?" Faraday didn't seem to care one way or

the other, as he sat down on the edge of the bed and rubbed his eyes.

"That's right, Faraday. My employers are all very sad people."

"Oh? Why's that?"

"Because they all lost loved ones. Women close to them who were killed. By you. They want justice, Faraday. They want to make sure you die the way you deserve. That's why they sent me to do the job. Vengeance is my specialty."

"I'm very impressed." Faraday yawned.

Sullivan had had enough of this arrogant killer's affectations. He was here to accomplish a mission and now was the time to finish it. He stepped forward, aiming to riddle the pretty boy's face with bullets, when Faraday suddenly grabbed one of the tall bedposts. The upper half detached instantly and the cunning psycho swung it like a baseball bat, knocking the Uzi from Sullivan's hand.

In that instant, the harmless college boy suddenly turned into the raving maniac Sullivan had expected all along. Spittle dribbled out of the corner of his mouth, and his laugh was high and unearthly, like a siren from hell. He sprang at Sullivan, smashing him over the shoulders with the ornately carved ball at the end of the heavy bedpost.

As Sullivan absorbed the first blow, he berated himself for taking the situation for granted. With all his experience, he should have known that nothing is ever as it seems and that there are no easy jobs.

Faraday was a crazed banshee, swinging his weapon with speed and accuracy. An expert blow behind Sullivan's knees sent him to the carpet. Sullivan rolled away and jumped to his feet as Faraday's death blow came crashing to the stone floor, splintering a chunk out of the wooden post.

Faraday probably had weapons stashed all over the suite, Sullivan figured. Not guns, though, but clubs, knives, machetes.

Sullivan glanced around the room for the Uzi, but Faraday smashed the bedside lamp, throwing the room into darkness. Only the few moonbeams shining through the rolling clouds illuminated the large room.

Sullivan could see the wiry silhouette of the psycho stalking him with his club. He circled toward the bed, willing to risk a hunch. When he got close enough, Sullivan reached out and grabbed the other post at the foot of the bed. It came away easily in his hand, just like the other one.

Sullivan took the four-foot post and squared off in the primary position of *rokushakubo*, Okinawan staff fighting. Faraday screamed his high-pitched laugh and did the same.

"Ah, so!" the psycho killer repeated over and over, mocking Sullivan.

Sullivan was through fooling around. He growled like a tiger and went to work with his weapon, blocking Faraday's club, then sending punishing blows to the killer's ribs and jaw.

But Faraday just kept screaming "Ah, so!" seemingly unaffected by Sullivan's offense. Among his other vices, Faraday had to be a drug addict, Sullivan guessed. He behaved like someone out of his mind on "angel dust," totally fearless and numb to all pain. Sullivan would have to bludgeon the killer to a bloody pulp to accomplish his mission.

A spear thrust to the brisket only sent Faraday leaping across the room like a monkey. He landed on the bed, jumping up and down, shrieking maniacally.

Just as Sullivan went to pursue, the partial cloud cover outside passed and the full moon shone brightly. He glanced toward the window; under one of the chairs was the Uzi. It was time to put this asshole away once and for all, he thought, as he lunged for the submachine gun.

Faraday bounded off the bed headfirst and jumped Sullivan just as he was within reach of the Uzi. Like most psychos, Faraday was much stronger than he looked and the angel dust had only made him more fierce.

"I'm a vampire!" he shrieked in Sullivan's ear, then sank his teeth into Sullivan's bicep, piercing his jacket with his incisors.

Sullivan shrugged him off and smashed the psycho's face with his other fist. His huge balled hand was like a wrecking ball, and he could feel the wetness of blood spurting out of Faraday's smashed nose.

Yet through the burble of blood filling his mouth, the psycho continued to laugh.

Sullivan reached up and grabbed the stock of the Uzi, but before he could get his finger on the trigger and point the muzzle, Faraday threw his full weight on Sullivan's arm and gripped the submachine gun.

"Give it to me!" Faraday shouted. "I need that! I can use it!"

Sullivan locked his grip on the gun. There was no way he was going to let Faraday have it. But he also knew there was no way that Faraday was going to stop his tugging. And with Faraday's knee cutting off the circulation in his arm, he didn't know how long he could hold on.

Summoning all his might, Sullivan heaved Faraday up and off, but in the process he lost his hold on the Uzi. Falling back on his ass, Faraday fumbled with the gun in his hands, trying to find the trigger.

Sullivan lunged, grabbing the Uzi by the muzzle and pointing it to the ceiling as a burst of fire strobe-lit the room. The hot muzzle burned Sullivan's hand, but he didn't let go.

As they struggled for the gun again, Sullivan recalled the angry stare of Angela Mills, the girl whose mother was executed by Faraday. He envisioned her slim, beautiful face, focusing on the anger and bitterness that Faraday had put in her beguiling eyes. He'd do it for her, for Angela Mills. Battling for possession of the weapon, Sullivan vowed to himself and to Angela Mills that Faraday would die by his hand if it was the last thing he did.

As the image of the young girl's face became clearer in his mind, Sullivan found new strength, and the gun started to slip slowly from the psycho killer's clawing grip.

9

An Unwelcome Interruption

Ten minutes before Sullivan's battle for the Uzi, Preminger had just pocketed the twenty thousand dollars cash that Jerome Faraday Sr. had paid him, and was about to leave when the billionaire swung around in his high-backed leather chair and looked him in the eye.

"Are you leaving Mexico immediately, Preminger?" Faraday asked abruptly.

"Why do you ask?"

"I could use you down here. You seem to be a capable man, certainly capable of using the brains you were born with."

"Cut the compliments, Mr. Faraday, and get to the point. You want me to work for you? Is that it?"

"Precisely." Faraday nodded curtly. "To be frank, I'm long on firepower here, but annoyingly short on brainpower. The men I've hired are common criminals. They take orders, but they have little initiative beyond that. I could use someone with your know-how to patrol the area, the town, the roads, et cetera. In other words, I want someone who will tip me off to trouble before it gets to my front door, as it were."

"Espionage isn't my thing, Mr. Faraday—"

"Nonsense, Preminger. This is no time for modesty.

I think you're an excellent snoop, and I need an advance warning system, as it were."

"Well, I don't—"

Faraday's mottled face turned crimson. "Don't be coy with me!" he exploded. "You'll get twenty-five hundred dollars a week plus expenses. Call me every day with whatever information you come upon. I have plenty of enemies and so does my son, so you'll surely hear something out there. Now, unless there are any further objections, I'll consider you on the payroll."

"Just one condition, Mr. Faraday."

"What's that?" the old man snapped.

"I leave this place right now. I don't want Sullivan to see me here . . . just in case your boys don't take care of him."

"You don't have to worry about the so-called Specialist. But if it will make you feel better, you may go. Take that way." Faraday pointed to the bathroom. "The door in there leads directly outside. No one will see you leave."

Faraday selected one of his solid gold pens and quickly scribbled something on a piece of paper. "Here, this is my number. Call me around three every afternoon. Now, go."

Preminger pocketed the phone number and slipped out through the bathroom exit.

Faraday bolted up from his desk and headed for the mess hall. If this Sullivan was as lethal as Preminger seemed to think, he'd have to be taken care of swiftly and finally. Faraday couldn't have his only son murdered by a soldier of fortune, a hired killer. It would be a social disgrace, a black mark on the family history. No, that just wouldn't do.

He rushed into the cobblestone courtyard, walking briskly for a man his age. The roses climbing the trellises along the arched walkways were fragrant on the warm moonlit evening, but Faraday was oblivious of such things. Only three things mattered to Jerome Faraday Sr. Power, money, and the Faraday heritage.

When Faraday burst into the mess hall, the men were well into their beers and tequila, laughing raucously, arm-wrestling, boasting, and challenging one another. The intoxicating bravado of Mexican *machismo* had them all under its spell. But Faraday was not intimidated. He stood in the middle of the room like a stern schoolteacher waiting for the class to settle down.

When Ludlow noticed the boss glaring at the uproar, he sobered up and yelled over the din. "Hey, shut up, you guys. Shut up, I said!"

Gradually the men began to feel Faraday's steely presence and they quieted down to a low grumbling.

"Is something wrong, sir?" Ludlow asked obsequiously.

Faraday scanned the faces around the room. "Where's Stark?"

"Stark? The new guy? Gee, I dunno—"

"He's in the can," K.C. called out, laughing.

"The can, my ass," Faraday snapped. "That man is an infiltrator, a hired assassin."

"What?" Ludlow screwed up his face.

"As I suspected, his name is not Stark. It's Sullivan. Jack Sullivan. He's also known as the Specialist."

Several jaws dropped at the mention of the Specialist.

"Shit!" Reece said, shaking his head. "That's one bad mother fucker. A killing machine. And he don't take no prisoners!"

"Hoo-wee!" Burke, the killer from Louisiana, exclaimed. "I know all 'bout that ole boy. He's the one who leveled the Blue Man's operation. Him, two other mercs, and this ole drunk Indian went up against a whole base full of trained terrorists . . . and won."

Faraday crossed his arms and scowled at the assembly. "I'm not at all interested in trading folklore about this character. I want you to find him and kill him *immediately*. Now, hurry up!"

No one moved. The ones who knew of Sullivan were petrified; the rest were naturally wary when they saw the reactions of the men familiar with the deadly killing force lurking somewhere within the *castillo*.

"Do I have to repeat myself, gentlemen?" Faraday's shrill voice pierced the room. "I want that man vanquished and I want it done now!"

"Just one second, Mr. Faraday," Ludlow began, pushing back the air in front of him with his palms. "I don't want no part of this Specialist guy. I've heard too much about him. I think I speak for everybody when I say—"

"Must I remind you, my friend, that you are in my employ?" Faraday's voice overrode Ludlow's protestations. "I'm paying you all fine salaries to protect my home."

"Yes, but this is an excep—"

"There are no exceptions, Mr. Ludlow. And if you choose to quit, I must remind you that the local *federales* are also in my employ. I guarantee that they will make sure you never leave this godforsaken jungle alive if you abandon ship now."

Faraday's voice reverberated through the otherwise silent mess hall. The men knew Faraday had the *federales* in his pocket, but they couldn't be sure how many of them there were. And the thought of fighting their way through the jungle seemed almost as bad as facing the Specialist.

Faraday sneered down at Ludlow. "Well, Ludlow, are you going to get him or not?"

The fat man exhaled deeply, looking to his key men, Reece and Jake. The hopeless look in their eyes told the story. They had no choice but to do what Faraday wanted.

"Okay, you win," he grumbled, "but we do it my way."

"Whatever you think is best," Faraday cooed with a condescending smile.

"Search parties of no less than three guys," Ludlow said officiously. "And we're not responsible for any damage done anywhere. Whoever spots the Specialist can do whatever he has to, to put him away."

"You're boring me with details, Ludlow. Just do it."

"Right," Ludlow snorted. "You guys know what to

do. Form groups and get started. And remember, once you see him, just start blasting away."

The men didn't seem any more confident, but they obeyed, each of them secretly hoping the Specialist had done what he came for, and was already making tracks. They formed groups and started combing the halls, hearts racing, weapons at the ready. Ludlow naturally took Reece and Jake in his party.

When Ludlow saw that K.C., as usual, was the odd man out, he ordered him to join Burke's team. "And since you got four guys, you go check out Junior's room." Ludlow snickered. "Unless you're too scared."

The good ole boy was about to tell Ludlow to go fuck himself, but he'd never backed down from a challenge yet, and he wasn't about to start now.

"No problem, boss," K.C. whispered to the cracker. "I talked to Stark, man. I don't think he's anything special. Faraday's got his head up his ass about him."

"That so?" Burke grunted. If their party found Stark and shot him full of holes, that'd sure shut Ludlow's fat face. "Okay," Burke announced so Ludlow could hear, "let's go get this Specialist character. Hell, it's four against one, and *I* don't take no prisoners neither."

They rushed down the hall—Burke, K.C., an ex-hit man for the mob named Sal, and another Florida killer named Chaz—heading for the stairway that led to the second-floor wing where Jerome Faraday Jr.'s suite was located.

Their footsteps sounded heavily on the thick red carpet, and their ill-kempt weapons clattered in their hands as they ran. They seemed fearless, a unified search-and-destroy steamroller, until they turned the corner and saw the empty staircase leading up to the second floor.

Suddenly they switched gears, going from the offensive to the defensive. They knew a man was supposed to be stationed here at all times. "Oh, shit . . ." K.C. mumbled as he spotted the trail of blood leading to the broom-closet door.

Burke rushed up behind him and whipped the door open.

The guard stared up at them cross-eyed; the single gash across his throat was a red, leering smile, and a sticky pool of blood had collected beside him.

"Well, I guess he's been here," Burke said evenly. "C'mon, let's go."

Burke ran up the steps, followed by his reluctant patrol. Maybe this Specialist guy really was as bad as they said.

When they reached the second floor, their fears were reconfirmed by the lifeless body of the black giant sprawled out in front of Jerome Junior's door.

The severed hand stopped K.C. in his tracks.

"C'mon dammit," Burke growled to Chaz and Sal. "He's got to be in here."

The three men rushed to the door to see Sullivan and Jerome Junior on the floor struggling for the Uzi. For a split second Jerome Junior stared at his father's hired killers like a cat caught in a car's headlights. The distraction was all Sullivan needed to wrench the sub-machine gun away from him. But in the next split second, Sullivan had to make a choice. Kill Jerome and be killed in turn by the men leveling their weapons at him. Or fire at the three guards and risk losing Faraday Junior. As it turned out, self-preservation was the stronger instinct.

The Uzi blazed. Burke and Sal fell; Chaz retreated. Faraday Junior scuttled into the next room. Sullivan turned to blast him, but the goddamn clip was empty. Just then, Chaz and K.C. appeared in the doorway, their weapons sputtering wildly.

Sullivan didn't like the odds. It was time to make his exit, and the window was his only option. As he crashed through the glass, leaving a glittering shower in his wake, Sullivan suddenly realized that there was a good chance he'd find a sheer 150-yard drop-off beneath him. A very quick trip to the jungle below.

But a narrow roof came between Sullivan and the big

plunge. He hit the roof hard but couldn't get a good foothold. He started to slide, the steaming black expanse ready to swallow him. His legs went over the edge, but he was able to hold on, hanging by his fingers from a terra-cotta gutter. Sullivan looked down into the dark maw of death and decided that he wasn't going to go that way. The gutter cracked in agony as he swung his 240 pounds onto the veranda under the roof. He hit the stone porch in a crouch, barely clearing the low wrought-iron guardrail.

No time to rest, though. Another killer clambered out of the garden bushes, beside the veranda, the silhouette of an automatic pistol in his hand. The man fired wild, wasting shots in the darkness. Sullivan crouched in the shadows, waiting for him to come a little closer. . . .

He lunged at the man, knocking him down hard. They both heard the gun skittering across the stone floor, becoming obscured in the darkness.

The killer sprang to his feet and drew a machete from his belt sheath. It glimmered evilly in the moonlight. "Okay, pal, give me the pleasure," the killer hissed. "I sliced off my patrol officer's head back in California. I'd love to do it again to you."

This revelation stoked the killing machine in Sullivan. The killer thought he was putting the scare into his opponent, but he was really doing just the opposite.

The killer swung his machete arrogantly, making it whoosh threateningly. What he didn't know was that Sullivan had a blade of his own, the hooked tempered-steel kukri.

Sullivan drew his weapon and sized up the situation. The only advantage the machete had over the kukri was that it had a longer reach, but Sullivan decided to take care of that right away, rushing the killer at the first opportunity and clashing blade against blade. The kukri's superior steel cut into the machete's blade. They locked horns like battling rams, wrestling for the better position.

The killer scratched and clawed at Sullivan's face. Sullivan had his thumb on the man's windpipe, squeezing, pressing, finally strangling the man with fingers like rolled steel, their blades locked uselessly at their side. The killer withered and fell to the floor with a dull thud.

Sullivan could hear the clamor of footsteps in the courtyard inside. More killers looking for him. He couldn't take them all on with just his knife. It was time to get the heavy artillery.

In the shifting moonlight he could see that there was a narrow path, no more than a ledge really, circling the outside wall of the *castillo*. If he slipped, he'd go over the edge, down the cliff, and into the jungle to die of his wounds or be eaten by scavengers. On the other hand, if he met up with more killers with automatic weapons on the path, he was also dead meat. But he had to take that chance. He couldn't stay where he was, and without a good weapon he was useless. Sullivan bolted for the path, ready to take his chances.

10

Rumble in the Jungle

Once Sullivan found his way back to the path he'd taken to get to the *castillo* that afternoon, he had little trouble locating the tree with the double slash marks that held his artillery. Working fast, he cut the rope and lowered the duffel containing the M79 grenade launcher and the CAWS machine-shotgun. He hauled the duffel over his shoulder and retreated farther into the jungle, feeling his way through the wet blackness before him. Faraday's men were beating the bush searching for him, and from the commotion they made, he guessed there were about a dozen of them.

These killers certainly weren't amateurs. They were all hardened criminals, borderline psychos, sociopaths, men who got a big thrill out of watching their victims bleed. They weren't soldiers and they certainly weren't team players, but now they were working somewhat systematically to find him. Sullivan knew that when renegades pull together as they had, they must want their target pretty bad.

Of course, anybody who'd protect slime like the Faradays wasn't exactly on Sullivan's Christmas-card list. He wanted them as badly as they wanted him.

He crouched down behind a stand of palms and watched the path. It wasn't long before three of Faraday's killers came down the trail, stalking the way all patrols in Vietnam did—one man on point, the second a few paces behind and to the side, the third bringing up the rear. Sullivan was impressed, but he doubted that they'd learned it in the service.

Three birds with one stone was awfully tempting. Sullivan slowly unzipped his duffel and pulled out the M79 grenade launcher.

The M79 was a small weapon with big firepower. It was only twenty-nine inches long, with a fourteen-inch muzzle, but it could deliver five .277kg. grenades a minute, with an effective range of 383 yards. Sullivan cracked open the breech and loaded the weapon, then moved stealthily through the undergrowth, heading back for the path where he could get off an unobstructed shot. He stopped when he could hear his targets down the path talking.

"I can't see shit in this fucking jungle."

"What're we doing here? Mr. Specialist can't survive out here. The snakes'll get him before he reaches the road back to Santa Celesta."

"Hey, assholes," Sullivan called to them.

The men stopped short and looked around. In the jungle, sounds seemed to come from everywhere.

When they were quiet for a full minute, Sullivan called out again. *"I'm talking to you, assholes. Or don't you know your own name?"* He'd make them talk so he could figure out exactly where they were. . . .

"Hey, look, man," the point man yelled, "you're outnumbered. Give yourself up now and save your ass."

Sullivan treated them to his demonic laugh. "You don't expect me to believe that you won't shoot me down if I come out, do you? Anyway, who says I'm outnumbered? There can't be that many of you."

"You're pretty fucking sure of yourself for someone out alone in the jungle at night," the point man said.

"Oh, I've got friends," Sullivan said, gritting his teeth. "Good buddies. Like this one."

He pulled the trigger and a grenade zoomed down the path like a flaring guided missile. The three thugs didn't have time to wipe their noses before they were just memories. Blood, entrails, and raggedly severed limbs splashed over the trail.

Sullivan trotted down the path to inspect the damage. He rested the stout weapon on his shoulder and smiled grimly.

He'd wiped out at least a quarter of the search party in one shot, but in doing so, he had given away his position and now the others would be closing in on him from all directions. Hiking the duffel back on his shoulder, he slipped into the jungle, stopping only to scoop up a handful of black soil, which he used to rub over his face and hands for camouflage.

As he moved through the shifting shadows of the steaming moonlit jungle, he suddenly heard movement—the shuffle of feet on jungle debris, perhaps. He spun and looked all around him, but he couldn't see anyone. That didn't mean that someone couldn't see him, though. Sullivan kept moving, vigilant for any unusual sounds or movements in the shadows.

He knew someone was out there watching him. But if the enemy could see Sullivan, why wasn't he firing?

Sullivan eased the duffel off his shoulder and slowly unzipped it. He needed firepower. Carefully he reached in for the CAWS automatic shotgun . . .

But before he could get the gun out of his duffel, the enemy made his move. A thug jumped out of the bushes, a commando knife gleaming in his hand. He lunged immediately and caught Sullivan on the forearm with his blade, piercing the sleeve of his bush jacket.

Sullivan gave no thought to his wound. If he did, he'd lose. Instead he went with the flow of the man's thrust, spun around 360 degrees, caught the man's wrist, and broke it over his knee like a dry stick. The knife fell from his hand and hit Sullivan's foot. Sullivan reached for it, but the thug kicked him in the kidney as he bent down. Sullivan winced and went down on one knee, but his eyes never left his opponent, who was now reaching for his pistol.

"You're a dead man, Specialist." The thug grunted with great satisfaction.

Gathering all his energy, Sullivan gripped the knife in his left hand as he leapt up, throwing his right arm around the man's neck and sticking him in the gut with his own knife. The man retched as Sullivan inscribed a triangle in his stomach as if he were carving the eye out of a jack-o'-lantern. The man wailed as his guts started to spill out. Sullivan let him fall.

Sullivan wasn't about to stick around now; he could hear the others moving in. It was time to retreat into the thick of the jungle. But as he went for his duffel, a figure flew out of the shadows and grabbed him from behind, locking him in a half-nelson. The attacker didn't count on Sullivan's incredible bulk and he couldn't hold onto his grip. Sullivan quickly whipped him off his back, throwing the man off.

The attacker was lithe, athletic, and undaunted, one of the strongest men Sullivan had ever fought. He bounced to his feet and threw himself on Sullivan again, diving headfirst into Sullivan's midsection. Sullivan saw it coming and he tensed his stomach muscles for the blow. The attacker's head hit what must have felt like a sandbag and did no damage, but he fought on, pushing Sullivan back and back until he had him pinned against a thick tree trunk. He thrust his head up into Sullivan's chin, knocking the Specialist's head back into the tree.

Sullivan was stunned, and the attacker took advantage of his condition, throwing his hands around Sullivan's eighteen-inch neck and squeezing with all his might. Sullivan fought for breath, reaching out for the man's throat, feeling with his thumbs for the windpipe, pressing in to cut off the air supply. It was a battle of raw strength and stamina. Whoever had the strength to hold out and hold on would snuff the other and survive.

All sound ceased except for the thump of Sullivan's heart and his own straining grunt. Sullivan had no way of knowing who was getting the better of whom. He could only concentrate on his thumbs and hope his trachea could hold out longer than his opponent's.

Suddenly a shot rang out, shattering Sullivan's intense concentration, and the man slumped to the ground. Through the haze, Sullivan could see a group of thugs fighting through the vines, weapon blasts stobe-lighting the night. They'd shot their own man by mistake. Sullivan gulped air, mentally forcing himself to gather enough strength to get the hell out of there before they realized their mistake and plugged him too.

Retrieving the duffel, Sullivan staggered into the brush, plunging into the thickest, darkest area he could find, determined to bull his way through any terrain that might slow him down. He pulled the CAWS machine-shotgun out of the duffel, and popped the safety as he ran. Slinging the duffel over his shoulder, he tried to forget that he hadn't field-tested the machine-shotgun. On paper, the CAWS was the perfect infantry weapon, the kind of weapon that would have made all the difference in Nam. An automatic weapon with all the lethality and accuracy of an old-fashioned twelve-gauge shotgun. But Sullivan knew you could wipe your ass with what they put down on paper. Combat performance was all that counted.

He saw the opportunity to test the CAWS up ahead.

In the next clearing one of Faraday's men stood at the ready with an M16 assault rifle, the standard-issue infantry weapon in Nam. The man was about thirty yards away, waiting for Sullivan to be flushed out of the brush by his buddies. He had clearly heard Sullivan coming because he lifted his weapon into firing position.

"Come on out, asshole, and give me a good shot at you." The cocky thug laughed, confident that Sullivan was trapped.

The M16 barked, spraying the brush all around Sullivan with slugs.

Now it was Sullivan's turn. As the enemy was shoving a fresh clip into his rifle, Sullivan lifted the CAWS and found the man's head in his sights.

"Kiss it good-bye, pal," Sullivan whispered as he pulled the trigger.

The twelve-gauge explosion ripped through the clearing. A second later, the savaged body of the rifleman toppled over. His head was pulverized, and the gory pulp had been smeared over the trees and bushes behind him.

Sullivan regarded the automatic shotgun with admiration. Field test completed, results positive.

He rushed through the jungle, passing the dead man's position and escaping farther into the thick of the jungle. They'd give up on him soon, and he'd have a night to rest up and plan his strategy.

Faraday Junior had slipped through his fingers, but the day hadn't been a total loss. Tallying up his hits for the day, he was pleased with the results. Eleven killers down, either snuffed or out of commission. That was roughly half of Faraday's force. Not bad for a day's work.

Now he had to figure out how he was going to get to the rest of them, especially Faraday and son. He'd have to give that some thought. It wouldn't be so easy the next time; they'd be on their guard, waiting for him.

But he couldn't plan anything now. He had to rest first and bandage that knife wound on his forearm. He plowed through the undergrowth, driving on like a tireless heavy-duty machine.

11

Teamwork

Sullivan kept mentally replaying the scene in Jerome Junior's room, where he and the psycho killer struggled for the Uzi. Again and again, he went over the events that led up to that fight, searching for some flaw in his plan, some mistake he'd made that allowed his target to escape.

He sat with his back to a tree, tying off the gauze bandage on his arm by the light of a small fire he'd built to scare off snakes, tarantulas, and nosy monkeys. The cut was minor, just a flesh wound, but the risk of infection was high in the jungle, so Sullivan wasn't going to take any chances. He'd washed it out with water from his canteen, then painted it with iodine before wrapping it with clean gauze. He pulled the last knot tight with his teeth, then leaned back and stared into the flames, looking for answers.

I underestimated Faraday, he thought bitterly. I should have learned by now. Never take anything for granted. There are no easy jobs. That was my mistake. I took these guys for granted. A bunch of ragtag thugs led by an old man protecting a killer of women. Sounded like a piece of cake, and I ate it. Killers are killers, and when they're attacked, they defend themselves the best way they know. By hitting back, hitting back hard.

The memory of those men calling him "the Specialist" in the jungle came back to him in the sinister quiet of the present jungle. He believed he was a specialist when he got the name back in Nam. You had to believe you were special in order to survive in combat. But Sullivan feared that maybe, just maybe, he was resting on his laurels a bit too much. He had to get back to basics. Stop hotdogging it, and run the plays by the book for a change.

He stared up at the moon peeking at him through the silhouettes of fronds and branches, listened to the agitated chatter of unseen monkeys. They didn't like having an intruder in their realm. Well, too fucking bad, Sullivan thought moodily.

This mood of dissatisfaction with himself was nothing new to Sullivan. It had happened like this before, and each time he had to knock himself down a peg before someone else did. He had to remind himself periodically that he was not invincible, that he couldn't do everything by himself. The first time he learned that was in Nam, in a jungle just like this, on that lurps mission to destroy that munitions depot near the Cambodian borderline.

It had been almost a week after Sullivan had single-handedly taken out the foo gas trap, slaughtering the four "bait" VC. Saving his men and destroying the enemy the way he did had put Sullivan on a real high. But that was bad. In Sullivan's case, it made him over-confident, cocky.

War is a team effort. Occasionally a soldier loses sight of that fact and tries to make it a solo event. You can get away with grandstanding and going it alone for a while. Once, twice, maybe even three times. And when that happens, you begin to believe that you're a hero. But then the time comes when you hang your ass a little too far over the edge, and that's when you get it blown off. Sullivan learned that lesson very well in Nam.

Lurps missions were as complicated as hell but as simple as could be, both at the same time. Simple because there was one goal, one target to hit, one village to liberate, something like that. Complicated because getting to the objective was never by the direct route. The enemy was always coming up with new tricks, stuff no one had ever heard of. And then there was the jungle, which was always a wild card. It could hide you or it could kill you, depending on how fate felt about you that day.

Plowing through the jungle in enemy territory, heading for the munitions depot, Sullivan had been good, very good at racking up the little victories. So when he got to the big enchilada, he was in the wrong frame of mind.

He'd never forget Simpson, the demolitions man he had on his team then. Lieutenant Simpson, who never took off his helmet because his carrot-red hair would have given the VC the best target they ever saw. Simpson the cautious, who was always figuring new angles and playing devil's advocate with Sullivan.

"You sure about this?" he had whispered to Sullivan as they watched the suspiciously quiet munitions depot from their covered position at the edge of the jungle.

"Damn, Simpson, what do you want? An invitation?" Sullivan growled. "We've been observing the area for seven hours now. Not a peep. Nothing. There's no one here."

"I don't know, Sullivan. I think we oughta wait some more. Fucking VC are shifty bastards, and this looks too easy. I think it's a trap."

Sullivan could have easily pulled rank on him and ordered him to obey, since he was in charge of this mission, but he respected Simpson for his rank and his expertise. Sullivan knew the man was dead wrong, and he was determined to show him his error.

"Why so nervous, Simpson?" Sullivan cajoled. "Why not just get this over with quick so we can get back to base?"

"It just doesn't look right to me," Simpson insisted. "Something's wrong here. I can feel it in my gut."

"Trust me, Simpson. The place is empty, because the VC think this area is secure. They don't expect infiltrators this far north. There may be a token guard inside, but we'll take care of them, chop-chop." Sullivan smiled and patted Simpson on the shoulder.

Simpson nodded reluctantly. He still wasn't convinced, but he was willing to give Sullivan the benefit of the doubt. Sullivan put together a plan, and within the hour he and his seven men emerged from the jungle and entered the compound.

There were four long corrugated-tin warehouses in the compound, and according to the air-recon reports, each one should be well-stocked with ammo, small arms, and explosives. Each man in Sullivan's unit carried blasting caps and hand detonators, and they all knew how to use the Russian- and Chinese-made grenades and land mines that they'd find in the warehouses. Two men were assigned to each warehouse. Their orders were to put together the most powerful blast they could with whatever was available, wire it to hand detonators, then meet back outside in the courtyard in fifteen minutes. Once everyone was accounted for, Sullivan would give the signal for destruction. By the time any enemy in the area spotted the fireworks, the team would already be in the jungle, heading south.

They entered the clearing cautiously, Sullivan himself taking point with his finger poised on the trigger of an M60 machine gun. The men fanned out to a V formation behind him, their M16's at the ready.

The humidity covered them like a wool blanket; the sky was gauze over the wounded sun. A bird trilled somewhere in the distance. The sound of their own feet padding through the high grass filled their helmets.

Sullivan surveyed the courtyard formed by the four warehouses. It was about thirty yards square and covered with gravel. Each building was identical: the same number of windows, same rusting tin walls, one doorway and one loading dock facing the courtyard. It was an eerie scene. Like being alone in a department store after-hours.

He gave the signal, and the men paired off and went to the doorways of their assigned warehouses. Simpson followed Sullivan to the warehouse to the far right of the courtyard, gravel crunching loudly under their boots. Sullivan noticed that Simpson still looked uneasy as he proceeded to kick in the door, which put up little resistance to his size-twelve steel-shank combat boot.

Sullivan rushed in muzzle-first, scouring all four corners for enemy presence. Nothing. Nothing but stacks of wooden crates loaded on pallets in the dim gray light that filtered through the grimy windows. Every crate was stenciled with a serial number and some kind of inventory data—half of the markings were in a Slavic language, the rest in Chinese characters.

"Well, Simpson, I guess it's time to go to work," Sullivan said, setting down the machine gun and unsheathing his tempered-steel commando knife.

Simpson didn't say a word, but the sweat pouring down his face spoke for him. He drew his knife and started prying open crates to see what they had to work with.

Nails squeaked and strained as they started ripping the lids off their first crates. Boards fell to the dirt floor; then silence. Simpson turned to look to Sullivan, his face dead white. "Mine's empty," he hissed.

"So's mine," Sullivan said. "Try one from that pallet," he ordered, pointing with his knife as he attacked another crate.

Again, two empties.

"Oh, shit, man," Simpson muttered, his voice high and scratchy. "We are in deep shit, man."

"Be coo—"

But before Sullivan could finish, glass shattered and AK47 muzzles flashed from broken windows, like fire-breathing snakes. It was an ambush. The "munitions depot" was another goddamned VC trap.

Sullivan dove for the M60 and let it wail. Bullets

riveted the tin walls, lines of holes swerving into all the windows. The muzzle snakes retreated, but he had no doubt they'd be back.

Simpson had taken shelter behind a stack of bogus ammo crates, firing random bursts from his M16. His face was twisted and pale, his shoulder bloody.

"You hit bad?" Sullivan shouted as he ran for shelter.

Simpson only stared at him with a dirty reproachful look in his eyes.

Sullivan deserved that. He had assumed it was safe, assumed that it was going to be a piece of cake. Never assume it's an easy mission, because easy missions don't exist. There are always complications, always complications.

But there was no time for apologies. His men were in danger, isolated and cut off from their leader. Sullivan had no idea how many enemy they were up against or what they had in store for them. There was no time for fancy strategy. The only thing that would save them now was balls.

Sullivan rushed along one wall to the nearest window and peered out. The courtyard was crawling with VC, two dozen of them that he could see. They were firing through the windows of the other buildings. Two runty-looking Charlie were fiddling with a Russian grenade launcher, aiming it straight at Sullivan's position. Quickly he snapped up the M60 and sent them spinning to commie heaven.

"Simpson," he yelled, "get your grenades ready. We're getting out of here."

Although his expression was blank and distant, Simpson responded immediately, pulled a grenade from his belt. Sullivan had faith in Lieutenant Simpson. He was a team player, he'd come through for them.

Sullivan turned to the rear of the warehouse, shoved a fresh clip into the machine gun, and fired, inscribing a six-foot gash into the flimsy wall. After he traced it over three times, he ran up to the wall, kicked the tin flaps open, and crashed through to the outside, spitting lead. There was no one guarding the rear of the building. But he did see how the VC accomplished the ambush.

Sod-covered hatches covering two-man holes were scattered all over the perimeter. Spider holes. Bolted to the hatches were radio receivers. The warehouses were wired. As soon as they'd heard Sullivan's men opening crates, they came out of hiding and attacked.

Sullivan ripped two grenades from his belt and handed them to Simpson. "You start lobbing these over the roof and into the courtyard. Keep them busy while I get our guys out."

Rainey and O'Keefe were in the next building. Sullivan had no way of knowing their location in there, or if they were alive. There was no time to find out. Without hesitation, he raised the machine gun and started to inscribe another gash. He just hoped to God that he wasn't plugging his own men.

Simpson sent two grenades over the tin roof, one right after the other. Staggered explosions, then VC shouts and screams carried back from the courtyard. Clearly they weren't expecting heavy retaliation. Maybe the VC made the mistake of assuming they'd be shooting ducks in a barrel.

Sullivan pried open his ragged-edged doorway, the sheet metal rumbling like thunder. He leveled the M60 at the windows inside and drove back the enemy muzzles. Rainey and O'Keefe crawled out from their position flat on their bellies behind a similar stack of bogus crates. They were okay.

"Get out of here, on the double," Sullivan snarled. But O'Keefe and Rainey didn't have to be told.

Sullivan leapt through his escape hatch just as a VC grenade came sailing through the window behind and clattered across the floor. He hit the ground tumbling. The explosion inside the empty tin structure was deafening. The wooden crates ignited instantly; fire poured out every exit. Debris rained down on Sullivan's back.

When Sullivan looked up, Simpson was looking at

him. The color was back in Simpson's face, and he flashed a big grin as he pulled the pin on another grenade and lobbed it over the burning roof. He gave Sullivan the thumbs-up sign.

Sullivan got to his feet and found Rainey and O'Keefe. "Follow me," he ordered. "We gotta make our move before Simpson runs out of grenades."

He slapped a new clip into the M60 and rushed toward the courtyard. There was no wind, so the smoke just hung over the area, providing Sullivan with enough cover to make an assault. "Keep your backs to the burning warehouse, run sidestep, and follow me to the next building," he ordered.

The three men took deep breaths and ran into the courtyard, firing on full-auto as they went to save their buddies. Two M16's and Sullivan's M60 provided enough firepower to form a protective wall for them. Once they got to the door of the next building, Sullivan planned to shoulder his way in. He realized that Floyd and Blake, the men inside, could mistake him for an attacking VC and blow his ass to hell, but this was no time to go by the book. He just had to take that risk.

"Blake, Floyd!" Sullivan shouted from the doorway. "Don't shoot, you assholes, it's me."

The men were waiting by the door. They were just about to rush out on their own, seeing the smokescreen. Floyd had taken a slug in the thigh, but he was able to hobble. When they saw Rainey and O'Keefe with Sullivan, the grim fear in their faces melted away. Six special forces against two dozen Charlie were pretty good odds, Sullivan figured with a twisted grin. All they needed was to get Mancini and Dodd out and they'd massacre the bastards.

But just as Sullivan's optimism sparked his energy reserves, VC fire pounded the tin wall behind them, forcing them to eat dirt. The smoke was clearing, and they were dangerously exposed. Heavy machine guns were blazing from two positions on the other side of the courtyard. VC snipers had taken positions on top of the building where Sullivan and Simpson had been. But where the hell were the rest of them? Sullivan wondered. Circling around to attack from behind, no doubt. And Simpson, that poor bastard, was all by himself back there.

Suddenly a horrible scream slashed through the din of the compound. All Sullivan could imagine was some dink cutting Simpson's liver out. He wanted to go to him, help him, but they were all pinned to the ground by the snipers.

Sullivan looked to Blake, the best sharpshooter on his team, who was squeezing off shots with little success. The VC snipers were well covered by the peak of the warehouse roof, leaving Blake without much of a target to shoot at. Sullivan was glaring at the snipers on the roof, trying to think of some way they could be knocked out, when the fires of hell suddenly billowed up behind that warehouse, and a gust of yellow-red flame swallowed the snipers whole. A chorus of bloodcurdling screams stopped all fire for a second.

Seeing that the snipers were out of the way, Rainey, O'Keefe, Floyd, and Blake scrambled for better positions. They'd find out how it happened later, when they had time for explanations. Their prime concern now was eliminating the two machine guns that were bearing down on them.

But as they were scrambling, Sullivan saw hell open its jaws once more, enveloping the machine-gunner to the right in savage flames. When the flames receded a moment later, there were two charred black bodies, one slumped over the machine-gun muzzle, both their backs spiked with flames.

Well, if the devil wanted to help them kill VC, it was all right with Sullivan.

"Draw fire, draw fire," Blake yelled from across the courtyard. He was in position to pick off the other machine-gunner. Sullivan hoisted the M60 and treated the Charlie gunner to a party pack of American-made lead. The VC muzzle swung toward Sullivan, firing wildly. Sullivan hit the dirt as a spray of bullets riddled the tin wall behind him. He kept firing from the prone position. Bullets kicked up dirt in front of Sullivan's face.

Then Sullivan heard the distinctive crack of a single shot fired from an M16. Enemy fire ceased. The muzzle of the VC machine gun swiveled slowly to the side. The gunner was slumped forward, blood and pureed brain gushing out of his eye socket.

Sullivan turned to Blake and gave him the thumbs-up sign. Blake returned the compliment with a toothy grin.

"Cease-fire! Cease-fire!"

Sullivan turned toward the voice yelling from the area of the VC position. Simpson emerged from behind one of the warehouses with a flamethrower strapped to his back.

"Look what I found in one of those spider holes," Simpson said with a big grin. "Nice of these boys to capture one of our flamethrowers and have it delivered here for us!"

Sullivan could only shake his head at the man he'd given up for dead. "Nice work, Simpson. Where are the rest of the VC?"

"Running for the nearest water hole to cool their singed asses." He laughed.

"You're number one, Simpson," Sullivan said as the other men gathered around.

"Wrong, Sullivan. The *team* is number one."

Sullivan leaned back on his duffel, recalling Simpson's words that day. He'd learned a lesson then. It was a lesson he'd be wise to keep in mind.

Only, now he had no team. Now he was a loner . . . unless he could get a certain message out.

The Mexican jungle, like the Vietnamese jungle, was never silent, but the night chorus of crickets, moving snakes, tropical birds, and monkeys lulled him to sleepiness. He intended to get with the drill in order to achieve his objective—first thing in the morning. . . .

12

Traitor-in-the-Box

Sullivan had started out at sunup, humping it on foot through the jungle, heading for the main road. He was rested and determined when he started out, and when he eventually found out that he'd been carrying a boa constrictor in his duffel for a couple of miles, the adrenaline was better than a good strong cup of coffee. Fortunately, the snake decided to come out for some air when Sullivan set the duffel down for a moment as he gauged his bearings. It had slithered in during the night and gotten pretty cozy with the M79 and the CAWS. Startled, Sullivan drew his kukri as the boa slipped out the three inches of open zipper. He went to cut its head off, then stopped. The snake hadn't done any harm. It just wanted to get out so it could get a bird or something to eat. He let it go.

It took Sullivan about two hours to get back to the paved road, clawing his way through the brush rather than returning to the path where Faraday's men would probably be looking for him. When he reached the road, he stopped and watched for a while. Walking back to Santa Celesta on the road wouldn't be wise. There were men out looking for him, and coming out in the open would just make it easy for them. Flagging down the next passing vehicle was out too; no telling who'd be in it. He decided to follow the road from the jungle's cover, preferring to contend with the tangle of vines, the mosquitoes, and the snakes than risk a firefight in broad daylight.

Sullivan hiked for about three-quarters of a mile until he spotted something peculiar up ahead. It was a clearing, manmade, maybe thirty feet square. He stalked closer for a better look and saw furrows of tall slender plants. Parked by the side of the road was an old rusty Ford pickup, its owner sprawled out in the shade. At first Sullivan thought the guy was the victim of a holdup on the road, but after closer inspection of the little garden in the jungle, he was able to piece the situation together.

Those slender plants were marijuana, presumably planted by the young *hombre* sleeping off his high. This was his own private crop hidden out here in the jungle so the *federales* wouldn't find it and demand a bribe. Sullivan approached and looked down at the dope farmer. He was totally unconscious, a stupid grin plastered across his face.

The Specialist shook his head. "What a waste," he murmured in disgust.

Sullivan went over to the truck. The key was practically rusted in the ignition. Obviously there was no need for much security out here in the jungle, and that was just fine with Sullivan. Hot-wiring was a pain in the ass, and it damaged the vehicle. Plus, it made it seem like car theft. When Sullivan took a vehicle, he preferred to think of it as a loan.

He threw his duffel onto the seat and noticed a rag on the floor. It was an old sackcloth Mexican peasant shirt that the dopehead used as a dipstick rag. Sullivan peeled off his bush jacket and threw the grimy shirt over his head. He walked back to the dopehead and picked up the straw slouch hat that had rolled off the man's head when he passed out.

"I'll be borrowing this for a while too," Sullivan said, pulling the broken hat down over his eyes.

He hopped into the truck, cranked up the engine, and sputtered down the road, heading straight for Santa Celesta.

It was almost siesta time when Sullivan arrived in Santa Celesta. Before he started making arrangements for a second strike on Faraday's *castillo*, he thought he'd take advantage of the situation and see if he could pick up any information about Faraday's troop strength in the area.

He guided the battered old truck through the center of town and parked it across the street from the police station, a stucco shoebox structure set apart from the village's few stores. He wanted to see if there were any familiar faces at the police station, so he pulled his hat down over his eyes, leaned back, and pretended to be taking his siesta as he watched the entrance to the building.

He waited that way, feigning sleep, for two hours. He had to drive hunger, thirst, fatigue, frustration, and boredom out of his mind—a skill he'd learned in Nam. There was no guarantee this surveillance would pay off in any way, but he figured since he'd have to wait for sundown before he could move freely through the town, sitting in a pickup was as good as sweltering in the jungle for the afternoon.

Not a soul came in or out of the police station all afternoon. Then at a quarter of two, a figure appeared in the doorway, squinting at the oppressive afternoon sunlight. It was the bearded *federal*, the leader of the trio who had tried to run him off the road the day before.

The *federal* scratched his beard, then hitched up his pants. He looked up and down the dirt road before he stepped out of the doorway. He seemed to be checking to see if anyone was watching him.

The *federal*'s worn black boots kicked up puffs of dirt as he walked toward the cluster of stores. When he got to the front porch of the one "big" establishment in town, the combination general store and cantina, he looked over his shoulder, then slipped quickly inside.

The man was up to something, Sullivan was sure. Quietly he opened the pickup door, got out, and strolled toward the cantina.

But Sullivan was also being watched. Crouched on the floor of his booth, Ramón, the beer vendor who'd sold Sullivan a can of Tecate the day before, tilted his head and watched the big stranger in the dirty peasant shirt walking across the dirt road. He was suspicious. There was something wrong about that big man, he thought. And when Sullivan circled around the cantina and didn't relieve himself against the wall, Ramón knew something definitely was not right.

Sullivan had stalked around the back to a low glassless window, its shutters closed but the slats open. The room inside was cluttered with cardboard boxes, steel drums, shelves full of canned goods—a typical storeroom. Off in a corner there was a small round table surrounded by four mismatched chairs. The table hosted a small lamp with a dented tin shade, three dirty shot glasses, and a two-thirds-empty bottle of tequila.

Two dim figures shuffled into the storeroom and took seats at the table. One was the bearded *federal*. The other was Russ Preminger.

As soon as Sullivan recognized the New York detective, bile rose in his throat and his fists clenched reflexively.

So that's how Faraday found me out. . . .

"Señor Preminger?" the *federal* asked cautiously. Clearly it was their first meeting.

"*Sí,*" Preminger answered coolly, pulling out a cigarette and taking his time lighting it.

They spoke in fluent Spanish, but that was no problem for Sullivan. He'd learned to understand the spitfire Puerto Rican Spanish he heard all over New York City. By comparison, Mexican Spanish was a snail-paced drone and easy to decipher.

"It is my understanding, *señor*, that we are to coordinate with you," the *federal* began formally. "Mr. Faraday informed me early this morning."

Preminger nodded, squinting as he took a long drag off his cigarette.

The *federal* didn't look pleased to be working with the new man, but he seemed resigned to his orders. "Well, as you may know, I am the chief of all police in this area. You will have our full cooperation, Señor Preminger, but I will tell you now, my men take their orders directly from me. I ask you to respect my system and go through channels."

"Don't worry about it, Capitan Torres. My job is to collect information and head off trouble for Mr. Faraday. If I think the situation requires any manpower, I'll call you and leave it in your capable hands."

The smirk on Preminger's face belied the sincerity of his words. He helped himself to a drink, then slid the bottle across the table to the captain, who reluctantly poured himself a tequila. In Mexico, it wasn't customary to drink with a man you distrusted, but while the captain was in Faraday's employ, he'd had to deal with many untrustworthy men—men just like himself.

"So, Capitan, do you have any information for me? Any unwelcome arrivals in Santa Celesta?" Preminger didn't plan to take this job or the local police very seriously, but for the salary Faraday was paying him, he was willing to go along with anything.

"As a matter of fact, Señor Preminger, there *is* a new arrival in town. A woman. She's been asking about the *castillo* and Mr. Faraday."

Preminger leaned forward. "A woman, huh? Do you know who she is?"

"No, not yet. So far, all we know is that she's young and very pretty. With fire in her eyes. Shall we arrest her?" Capitan Torres asked humbly, mocking Preminger's authority.

"By all means, Capitan. If she's as pretty as you say, I want to meet her." The cigarette danced between

Preminger's lips as he reached to pour himself another
drink.

"Very well. I'll call my men and tell them to pick her
up." The *federal* got up to go to the phone in the front
of the cantina.

Sullivan had heard enough. A corrupt cop and a
two-faced private dick working to shield a psycho-killer.
That's all he needed to know.

Stealthy as a cat, Sullivan opened the shutters and
climbed up on the sill. In the blink of an eye, he
sprang, hurtling his 240 pounds at the scruffy *federal*,
knocking him on his face. Preminger stood up, surprised and unprepared. Instinctively Sullivan's foot
plowed into Preminger's gut, knocking the wind out of
him and temporarily neutralizing him.

Capitan Torres was back on his feet, reaching for his
9mm Beretta. Sullivan struck like a sidewinder—his
knee to the officer's groin—and the pistol fell from
Torres's hand, clattering to the wooden floor. Sullivan
stooped to pick it up and noticed Torres pulling a
stiletto out of his boot. He knew the captain's intentions
as if they were his own. Flick the blade and thrust, an
underhand cut straight into Sullivan's chest.

But in the split-second it took Torres to locate the
spring button on the stiletto, Sullivan scooped up the
Beretta and fired. Torres fell flat on his ass and landed
with his back propped against the door to the cantina.
A neat dime-size hole in the middle of the man's forehead oozed a rivulet of blood down the side of his nose
and into his thick black beard.

Sullivan whipped around to find Preminger making
his move for the window. "Freeze, Preminger," he
barked, leveling the gun at the detective's chest.

Preminger thrust his hands up in surrender.

"Turn around, slow," Sullivan ordered. Holding the
Beretta point-blank to Preminger's heart, he frisked
him and came up with a snub-nose .38. He tossed it
across the room behind a stack of boxes. Then, to
Preminger's shock, Sullivan threw his own gun down.

"There's nothing I hate more than a traitor," Sullivan growled, his keen eyes boring holes into Preminger's skull. "Death is too good for a traitor."

In Spanish, there is a term used for men with pugilistic skills like Sullivan's. Hands of stone. But if Preminger could have gotten enough breath under his broken ribs to utter anything through his bloody, swollen lips, he would have simply called it *pain*.

Sullivan's arms worked like mad-bull pistons, savaging Preminger until his face looked like a cherry pie that'd been run over by an eighteen-wheeler. It took all the control Sullivan could summon to stop himself before he killed the bastard. He might, just might, be useful later. Except for that, Sullivan had no reason to spare the man who'd betrayed all the families—his supposed "clients"—who'd lost wives, daughters, and mothers to Jerome Faraday.

Searching through the merchandise stored in the back room, Sullivan found a case of clothesline cord. He opened two plastic-wrapped packages and went to work tying up the semiconscious traitor. He bound Preminger tight at the ankles, knees, wrists, and elbows so that he couldn't budge. Then he balled the clear plastic wrapping and stuffed it into Preminger's bloody mouth, looping the rope tightly around his face twice.

Locating a large wooden crate, Sullivan proceeded to rip it open with his bare hands. He removed the four gas engines that were packed inside and hid them in other cardboard boxes. Then he dragged Capitan Torres's body over and dumped it in the crate. Preminger came next. It was a tight fit, but Sullivan made it work, forcing the lid down again and again until it shut. Finally he kicked a hole in one of the slats so that Preminger would have air.

"Sit tight, Preminger," Sullivan muttered as he leapt out the window. "I *may* come back for you."

13

Mexican Standoff

As soon as Sullivan's feet hit the dirt outside the cantina, the rigid steel muzzle of another Beretta 92SB gouged his kidney from behind. He turned his head and out of the corner of his eye saw a mean-faced *federal*—broken nose and blueberry lips topped by a crumpled peaked hat. Sullivan raised his hands and put on an amiable smile.

"*Qué pasa, amigo?*"

The question was answered with an incomprehensible bark and a hot cloud of chili breath. Sullivan turned away from the man's rancid smell as he considered his position. If this guy had heard the gunshot that killed his captain, he was probably checking out a suspicious character as any good lawman would. But it was clear to Sullivan that Santa Celesta had no good lawmen. So the question was, did he actually see Sullivan off Capitan Torres or not? If he did, Sullivan knew the man was certainly contemplating a swift execution.

"Now, listen, amigo—" Sullivan began.

"Shut up," the *federal* shouted. Sullivan could understand that much of his Spanish. "I am in control here!"

"Not exactly." Another voice in Spanish somewhere behind Sullivan's back.

The *federal* cursed someone's mother, and Sullivan turned around to see what was going on. There was a revolver poised eight inches from the *federal*'s ear. The gun was practically an antique, a Smith and Wesson .32 Hand Ejector, the first side-swing cylinder revolver ever made.

Sullivan arched his head back to see who was holding the old gun.

"*Buenas tardes, señor.*" It was little Ramón, the beer vendor. "This, *señor*, is what is called a Mexican standoff."

"I think I've heard of it," Sullivan said, his hands still poised in the air.

"Do not worry, *señor*," Ramón assured him. "This amigo may be a dumb ox, but he is not stupid. He would like to live, I think."

"Same here," Sullivan said wryly. "I take it the 'dumb ox' doesn't understand English."

"Of course not."

"Well, that's one thing in our favor."

"Please, *señor*," Ramón said confidently. "You can trust me. When I tell you it's okay, you may turn around, take this fool's gun, and give it to me."

"Why should I give it to you?"

"Because mine is an old piece of shit that hasn't fired a bullet in thirty years. I want a new one."

"Sounds reasonable to me," Sullivan muttered.

The *federal* yelled for them to speak Spanish and explain what they were saying. Ramón yelled back harshly, ordering him to shut up and give up his gun if he ever wanted to see his children again. Ramón punctuated his statement by jabbing the muzzle of his revolver into the man's scalp.

"Okay, *señor*, you may turn around and take my new gun." Ramón grinned.

But just as Sullivan was about to grab the *federal*'s Beretta, a second *federal* jumped out from around the corner of the building. His Beretta 92SB was leveled at Ramón.

"What do you call *this*?" Sullivan asked.

"A big problem," Ramón replied evenly.

The second *federal* yelled for Ramón to drop his gun, and Ramón yelled back that he'd kill his pal if he tried to shoot. This exchange went on for a minute or two before Sullivan said, "Tell me something, Ramón. Does this new guy understand English?"

"Not much."

"Well, we'll just have to take our chances that he doesn't understand what I'm going to tell you."

"As you Yankees say, 'I'm all ears!'" Ramón said, now as stiff-necked as the *federal* at the end of his gun.

"Good. I want you to tell them that it's me you want to shoot. Tell them that I raped your sister and that you must avenge the crime yourself."

"But, *señor*, I have no sister."

"All right, tell them I raped your mother."

"My mother is dead, God rest her soul."

Sullivan grimaced. "Do you have a pretty cousin?"

"Oh, yes. She is a virgin," Ramón said.

"Not anymore. Tell them I raped her and you want to kill me yourself. See if they buy that."

Ramón was a surprisingly good actor. He convincingly ranted and raved to the two *federales*, demanding his right to slay the pig who had disgraced his family. The *federales* gradually relaxed their positions, upon hearing his story. It was the kind of situation Mexican men understood very well, for Ramón had to assert his *machismo* and do what a man has to do when his honor is insulted.

"Remember, be angry when you talk to me now," Sullivan instructed. "Are they buying it?"

"I think they are," Ramón whispered. "Yes."

The second *federal* pointed his gun away from Ramón and toward Sullivan. Now there were two Berettas and a useless .32 aimed at Sullivan's back.

"Okay, now I want you to show them your gun. Tell them that it's no good and ask if you can borrow one of theirs to execute me."

"*Señor*, they are fools, yes, but they would never—"

"Just do it," Sullivan insisted.

"As you wish," Ramón muttered.

Ramón started to explain the state of his weapon to the *federales*. He seemed to be making a long story of it, engrossing the two men in his tale. Then he showed them his old Smith and Wesson, popping the cylinder, which comically fell out into his hand. The *federales* started to laugh. It was the distraction Sullivan was waiting for.

With almost superhuman speed and accuracy, Sullivan turned and struck, hammering the *federales'* gun hands with his fists. One Beretta hit the dirt, but the other man held onto his weapon. But before the *federal* could raise his gun, Sullivan had grabbed his wrist and bent it back, forcing the man to discharge his weapon against the stucco wall.

The other man reached down for his gun. Sullivan kicked it out of reach, then grabbed a fistful of greasy black hair and whipped the man into the wall. The stucco cracked, and the *federal* crumbled to the ground.

Ramón scrambled for the Beretta in the dirt as Sullivan continued to struggle with the conscious *federal*, who would not let go of his gun, fighting to point the muzzle at any part of Sullivan. Battling toe-to-toe, the *federal* kneed Sullivan in the groin, but Sullivan knew how to endure the worst of pain and make it work for him. Pain made him mad, and when he was mad, he was deadly.

Sullivan abruptly wrenched the man's arm into the air, spun around, and yanked the twisted arm down over his shoulder, tearing sinew and straining bone until the stubborn Mexican released his grip on the gun. After the gun fell, Sullivan's pistonlike elbow shot back and broke a rib or two. As the man gasped for air, Sullivan spun back around to face him. Double knife-hands to the pressure points where shoulder met neck—and the *federal* slumped like a body without bones.

Ramón stood off to the side admiring his new gun, wiping off the weapon's dust with his shirttail.

"Thanks for the help," Sullivan said, catching his breath.

"Huh . . . oh, you are very welcome, *señor*." Ramón smiled.

"Tell me something, Ramón. Have you seen any strangers in town since yesterday? A woman?"

"A young woman, very pretty, yes," Ramón said, whistling.

"Who is she? Do you know?"

Ramón shrugged. "She is American, I know that. She buy a drink from me and asked me where she could find a hotel. I told her there was only one place to stay in Santa Celesta, Ortega's Motel, out on the road into town. You must have passed it yesterday when you came in."

"Right," Sullivan said distractedly. He was thinking about this girl. Who the hell was she and why did Capitan Torres and Preminger think she was worth rousting? Bonnie wouldn't be stupid enough to follow him down here, would she? Whoever she was, it was clear that she'd be a target for Faraday's men. Sullivan had to find her before they did.

The motel was about three miles away on the narrow mountain road that led into the valley where Santa Celesta was located. He'd need a good vehicle just in case he had to perform a rescue, and the old pickup he'd taken from the pothead wouldn't do.

"Ramón, I need a good vehicle, preferably something with four-wheel drive. Got any suggestions?"

Ramón crooked his finger and led Sullivan around the corner of the building. He pointed to a shiny-new brick-red Jeep CJ. "Belong to Mr. Faraday. His new man, the spy, drive it into town last night. Do you like?"

Sullivan regarded the little man with a wry grin, marveling at what an asset Ramón had turned out to be.

"It has many advantages, *señor*," Ramón continued, like a used-car salesman. "Four-wheel drive, air conditioning, nice and clean—"

"And I have to hot-wire the goddamn thing," Sullivan muttered.

"No problem, *señor*."

Ramón shoved his new gun into his pants and walked over to the Jeep. He got in on the driver's side and stuck his head under the dashboard, feet dangling out the side. Sounds of metal scraping against metal, then silence. Twenty seconds later, the powerful six-cylinder engine roared to life.

"Not bad, Ramón."

"What you mean, not bad?" Ramón was indignant. "I was a legend in Mexico City when I was a boy. They called me the Scourge of the Zona Rosa."

"I apologize, Ramón. You're the best."

Ramón smiled proudly at the compliment as Sullivan got behind the wheel and slammed the door closed.

"Listen, Ramón," he said, putting a thousand-peso note into Ramón's hand and the Jeep into gear, "thanks for the help. If you happen to pick up any information about Faraday and his men, I'd appreciate it if you'd save it for me."

"*Señor*, I would be honored to help you rid this jungle of these animals."

"Great." Sullivan gave Ramón the thumbs-up sign as he pulled away, kicking up dust as he headed for Ortega's Motel.

The Jeep whined as Sullivan pushed it up the steep mountain pass to the motel that overlooked the valley and the impenetrable jungle below. He drove hard, unconcerned with whatever damage he might do to Faraday's Jeep, obsessed with thoughts of Bonnie Roland, luscious Bonnie. He was surprised and a little annoyed with himself that he felt so strongly about her. He hadn't felt this way about a woman since Lily. . . .

God damn that woman, he thought, getting madder by the minute. I told her not to interfere with my work. Fuck her women's-lib bullshit—merc work just isn't safe. And what the hell did she do with Melinda? She's supposed to be in New York watching the kid. . . .

Sullivan was as hot as the Jeep's radiator when he turned the bend and spotted the motel carved into the mountainside on the left. It was a two-story stucco affair, ten rooms at the most. The setting sun cast a rose-colored glow over the building. Even the white rooster scratching up dirt in the unpaved parking lot looked pink. Sullivan took note of the cars parked out front—three beat-up American-made sedans and the same Toyota Land Cruiser that had intercepted him when he arrived in Santa Celesta.

He pulled the Jeep to the side of the motel, where it couldn't be seen. His first impulse was to go in blasting, but he nixed that plan. They had a hostage, and there were probably innocent people inside who could get hurt in the crossfire. He turned the Jeep around so that its nose faced the road, just in case he had to make a quick getaway. As he opened the door to climb out, he spotted three khaki-uniformed *federales* leaving the motel.

Handcuffed and struggling in their grip was the woman in question. It was Angela Mills, one of the people who'd hired him for this mission, the college girl whose mother had been butchered by Faraday Junior.

Sullivan always demanded one condition whenever he took a job. The client had to agree not to help or interfere with his work—ever. Angela Mills was interfering, and her presence here was just an unnecessary complication. Complications, always complications. . . .

Lustrous black hair flying, Angela spat curses at the men. Ignorant of what she was saying, the determined *federales* forced her into the back of the Land Cruiser, one getting in with her, a pistol pointed at the small of her back. The other two jumped into the front seat.

As soon as the Land Cruiser tore out of the parking lot and headed back toward Santa Celesta, Sullivan knew they were going to take Angela to Faraday's *castillo*. The old man would interrogate her, have his thugs rough her up, and when they were through with her, they'd hand her over to Jerome Junior so he could have his jollies. The scenario burned Sullivan's gut.

No way, he thought. Angela Mills will not die at the hands of the man who killed her mother. No, they won't make it to town, not if I have anything to say about it.

He pulled from his waistband the Beretta 92SB he had taken from one of the *federales* behind the cantina. It held a fifteen-round clip, and only one shot had been expended in the fight. Fourteen bullets were more than enough to take care of the three corrupt cops. He popped the safety with his thumb, then wedged the gun into the crease of the passenger seat where he could reach it easily. Ramming the stick into first, Sullivan tore off in pursuit of the Land Cruiser.

14

Another Complication

The Land Cruiser raced down the treacherously narrow mountain road, a wall of jagged rock on the right, a sheer dropoff on the left. Pursuing in Preminger's Jeep CJ, Sullivan could see the heads of the two crooked *federales* up front and the third *federal* in the back. Angela Mills couldn't be seen. The guy in the back was probably holding a gun in her ribs to keep her still on the floor. Sullivan floored the accelerator. He was mad, mad at the corrupt cops working for Faraday and mad at Angela for getting in the way of his mission.

His head pounded as he discarded plans of attack. Without Angela, he could easily get rid of the *federales* by forcing their vehicle off the cliff. He couldn't open fire on them for fear of hitting her, or causing an accident by killing the driver. But he also couldn't let them get into town, where they'd have reinforcements.

It was three miles more or less to the center of town. Sullivan had to make his move in that three miles.

He'd have to cripple their vehicle somehow and force them to stop. The obvious solution was to shoot out the tires, but on the narrow road he couldn't pull alongside to get off a good shot. Unless . . .

"What the hell," Sullivan muttered to himself. "It's not my Jeep."

He reached for the pistol on the seat beside him and aimed at his own vehicle's windshield. The shot inside the Jeep was deafening; instantly the windshield turned into an intricate spiderweb mosaic. The second shot blew out the entire window except for some ragged fragments around the edges.

He was free to shoot right-handed. Putting the pedal to the metal, he bore down on the Land Cruiser, intent on stopping it.

Having heard the shots, the *federales* finally realized they were being pursued. Ignoring the dangerous condition of the road, the *federal* driver rammed the Land Cruiser into fourth and sped on. Their speedometer quickly registered sixty as they skidded around curves, coming dangerously close to the edge on each turn.

Sullivan was doing seventy, his nose right on the target vehicle's tail. He drove by instinct, hugging the edge, as he aimed the Beretta at the Land Cruiser's rear-outside tire. He squeezed off a shot that hit the dirt just short of the tire, and it occurred to him that he'd have to be careful not to hit the gas tank.

He tried to concentrate on his marksmanship, but the commotion inside the Land Cruiser distracted him. The *federal* in the front passenger seat jumped into the back. Angela still couldn't be seen. Then the Land Cruiser's back window suddenly exploded as the two *federales* started firing at Sullivan.

The road was too narrow to allow Sullivan to effectively outmaneuver the *federales*, and under the circumstances, blowing out their tires wasn't as easy as it first seemed. A bullet then zinged into the Jeep and punctured the seat back on the passenger side. Sullivan was getting impatient.

"No time to fool around with you," Sullivan grunted. Ducking under the dashboard, he floored the Jeep and rammed the Land Cruiser from behind. The jolt was enough to scare the *federales* for a second. Sullivan took advantage of the momentary cease-fire and peered over the dash. Still no sign of Angela. Good. They weren't smart enough to use her as a hostage. He noticed that the road up ahead was a little wider and that there was a pocket carved out of the rock on the right. Sullivan realized it was now or never. He'd have to take a chance that Angela would be safe in her crouched position.

Ignoring the bullets, Sullivan sat up behind the wheel. He swung the Jeep as far to the left as he dared, tire treads hanging over the crumbling edge of the cliff, then pulled back quickly and rammed the Land Cruiser again. The Jeep's grille crumpled against the Land Cruiser's left taillights, bumpers locking. Sullivan steered right; the Land Cruiser slid helplessly into the rocks, destroying the bodywork on the Cruiser's right, shearing off the front fender.

Sullivan held the wheel steady, staying with them like a cowboy bringing down a Brahman bull by the horns. The Land Cruiser veered into the pocket in the cliff and smashed head-on into a wall of rock. The driver's head went through the windshield as falling rocks dented the roof.

Sullivan's chest broke the Jeep's steering wheel upon impact, but there was enough steering wheel intact to keep going. Not even thinking about his bruised chest, Sullivan threw the Jeep into reverse and spun his wheels to disengage from the Land Cruiser. Metal strained against metal. Finally the Jeep's bumper gave way, tumbling loose to the dust as the Jeep flew back.

Sullivan slammed on the brakes, but the Jeep slid in the soft dirt and the rear-left wheel went over the edge with a pronounced *thunk*. He threw it into first and put his faith in four-wheel drive. The tires spun, digging holes in place; then Sullivan let up on the gas a bit and the treads bit into the road and pulled the loose wheel back from the brink.

Gunfire plinked into the side of the Jeep. The *federales* were firing at him again. Sullivan decided they were too close for comfort now, so he gunned the engine and hightailed it down the road and around the next bend.

Rounding a second bend, he came to another pocket where he was able to turn the Jeep around. He shifted back into first, with the Beretta resting on top of the stick in his hand. The engine coughed and choked as he threw it into second, rumbling back up the incline. Finally it picked up speed and Sullivan propped the muzzle of the Beretta on the dashboard.

"Come on out, amigos," he growled. "I'm ready for you."

Two *federales* were waiting for him, crouched in the middle of the road, guns at the ready. They opened fire on him, but he kept on coming. It was a battle of wills.

Slugs ripped into the Jeep, one grazing Sullivan's scalp slightly, just over his right ear. He didn't flinch, continuing to squeeze off shots as he aimed the Jeep right at them.

As the Jeep approached, the *federales* split. One went toward the edge while the other hugged the rocky wall. They thought Sullivan would pass like an angry bull and they'd be able to plug him as he passed. But Sullivan anticipated their strategy.

He turned the wheel and squashed one *federal* against the rocks like a bug while simultaneously leveling the Beretta out the passenger-side window at the other *federal*. His first shot only grazed the man's shoulder; his second got him in the chest. He pulled the trigger to finish the job, but the clip was empty—and the wounded *federal* still had his weapon in hand.

Clutching his chest, the *federal* fired wildly, staggering back in agony. He might have gotten Sullivan if he hadn't backstepped over the edge. His screams echoed through the sky as the dark jungle below swallowed him whole.

Sullivan knew that if the fall and the bullet wound didn't kill him, some boa eventually would. But that was the *federal*'s problem. Sullivan climbed out of the steaming Jeep on the passenger side and located the squashed *federal*'s pistol in the dirt. There was one more to take care of back at the scene of the "accident."

Sullivan stalked along the cliff, hoping to sneak up on the last *federal*, but when he got back to the Land Cruiser, all he found was the wreckage and Angela Mills struggling to get out of the vehicle, her wrists handcuffed behind her.

Sullivan whipped open the door and glared down at the girl. Her breasts were straining to get out of her tight blue chambray shirt. Her dark eyes were burning with vengeance lust, much more than they had back at Preminger's office in New York.

"Where's the other guy?" he yelled at her.

"He ran off," she shouted back angrily. "Up the road," she indicated with her head.

Sullivan was so mad he could have bitten the door off. Her interference was a definite setback in this mission. Right now, that *federal* was running to the nearest phone to call Faraday and tell him what had happened. Faraday's cadre would be out looking for him within a half-hour. So much for his surveillance plan.

"What the hell are you doing here?" he growled at her.

"Help me out of this heap," she snapped back. "And stop yelling at me."

"You're lucky I'm only yelling, honey." He reached in and pulled her out by the arm, his rough fingers squeezing her supple skin.

"Get me out of these things," she demanded, squirming impatiently in the handcuffs.

Sullivan didn't like her tone, but since he had been planning to free her anyway, he did as she asked. "Kneel down," he ordered, pushing her to the dirt.

"What?" she protested.

"Just shut up and do it."

"No! I don't have to—"

"Listen," he interrupted, "we don't have the key. I

have to blow them off. And unless you want the bullet to hit metal and ricochet up your ass, you'll get as close to that tire as possible."

She exhaled in annoyance, then did as he said, contorting her body so that the chain of the handcuffs rested flush against the already flat tire. Sullivan positioned the Beretta and fired at point-blank range, mangling two of the links. The acrid stink of burning rubber filled the air, but the tire harmlessly absorbed the bullet.

"You're welcome," he said sarcastically when he saw that no thank-you was coming.

"All right, thanks, Sullivan. You satisfied?" She scowled at him.

"No, I'm not satisfied. We had an agreement. You are not supposed to get in my way. That's part of the deal."

"Fuck the deal!" she screamed. "Faraday killed my mother! And I'm going to kill him!"

Sullivan wasn't going to bother arguing with her. Instead, he grabbed her arm and started to lead her down the road.

"Let go!" She pulled away from him.

"I've got no time for your bullshit. There are going to be others out looking for us, thanks to you. Now, let's go." He gripped her arm again and led her back to the Jeep.

The smell of boiling coolant hung over the road around the Jeep. "Get in," he ordered. "Just pray that this wreck holds out for a few more miles."

They got in and he attempted to start it with the wires Ramón had stripped back in town. The engine groaned but wouldn't turn over.

"Out," he ordered. "Let's try their truck. And pray harder this time."

They raced back to the Land Cruiser. When Sullivan turned the ignition, it started, then choked out. He tried it again, and the engine turned over. He took the Beretta out of his waistband and stuck it between his seat and the transmission hump, then pressed the clutch and put it in reverse. The Land Cruiser screamed for mercy, but Sullivan wasn't in a forgiving mood. He managed to turn it around and started up the road, fighting the wheel to keep the vehicle on the road as he rode the flat on its rim.

"At least we can make it back to the motel," he muttered.

She refused to answer him, moodily staring out the window. The sound of rubber flapping against the dirt road filled the silence, but the tension between them was thicker than the jungle humidity. Sullivan was still seething, and his head throbbed slightly from the *federal*'s slug. He wanted her gone. Now.

"After we get back to the motel, you're going to get your bags and get the hell out of Mexico. Immediately," Sullivan ordered.

"The hell I am," she sniped.

"You don't have a choice, honey."

She snapped her head around and glared at him hotly. "Do I have to remind you who you're working for, Sullivan? You're working for me, and I give the orders."

Sullivan slammed on the brakes and stuck his face in hers, the scar across his cheek white with anger. "I don't work for anybody, sweetheart! I work for justice, and I work alone. And when I do have help, it's not from amateurs. Am I coming in loud and clear?"

She flashed an arrogant smile at him, as if she knew she was holding the hidden ace. "Then I take it, Mr. Sullivan, you're willing to forsake the balance of your two-hundred-thousand-dollar fee."

Sullivan gritted his teeth, his nostrils flaring. "Honey, you can take that two hundred grand and cram it up your ass!"

He gunned the engine and wrenched the wheel, forcing the wounded Land Cruiser up the dusty hill back to Ortega's Motel.

15

A Troubled Mind

They continued up the road, unable to do more than ten mph on the flat tire. But with the intense resentment Sullivan and Angela Mills had toward each other, the trip back to Ortega's Motel seemed interminable. Sullivan felt like a lame duck in the limping Land Cruiser, slow and saddled with an ornery woman. And on top of everything else, there were probably men out looking for them right now.

"Shit," he mumbled to himself.

"What did you say?" Angela snapped.

Sullivan ignored her sharp question. He'd spotted something as he turned the bend. It was the third *federal*, hiking up the road. The man was limping, he'd probably hurt his leg in the crash, and his head leaked blood from its impact with the windshield. He couldn't have gotten to a phone yet, Sullivan realized.

Quickly he reached down to the floor, grabbed the peaked cap that had been discarded in the fray, and put it on. "You get down," he ordered Angela. "Don't let him see you."

Amazingly, the girl cooperated.

The *federal* was grimacing with the pain in his leg as he turned around to see the Land Cruiser crawling up behind him. Squinting into the sun, he waved to Sulli-

van, thinking one of his comrades had arrived to rescue him. Sullivan played along, pulling the Land Cruiser
to the left so that the man could get in on the passenger side.

"Be cool," Sullivan said to Angela through clenched
teeth. "He's coming up to the door now."

But when Sullivan reached for his gun, he only felt
air.

Suddenly Angela popped up like a jack-in-the-box
with the Beretta clutched in both hands. In that moment the *federal* realized that these weren't his buddies,
and his mouth opened to a soundless oval of shock and
fear. She opened fire, squeezing off shots with mea-
sured premeditated malice, aiming for the man's face,
chest, gut, and groin. She didn't stop until the *federal*
had fallen back over the edge of the cliff.

His body hit the trees, breaking branches and shaking leaves. There was no scream, though. He was dead
before he went over the edge.

"I hate men." She shoved the gun back where she'd
found it.

"That's healthy," Sullivan said dryly. "Faraday Junior
does what he does because he hates women."

"It's not the same. I could never do what he's done.
Not in a million years."

"Oh?" Sullivan put the Land Cruiser into gear and
watched the road ahead.

"I was the one who found my mother's body." Angela was suddenly talkative. "I told you what the papers
called her, didn't I? The Hamburger Lady. When I saw
her body in the garage, I didn't even recognize her. All
I could think of were those nature documentaries on
TV where lions and tigers catch gazelles, then tear
them up so bad they're just bones and bloody scraps of
meat. That's what my mother looked like. I thought a
bear had caught a big dog or a deer and mauled it
in our garage. But there are no bears in southern
Connecticut."

The hard edge had disappeared from her voice. She

just wanted to talk now, wanted to let out what had been pent up inside her for a long time. Sullivan decided to let her talk.

"I had just gotten home from college. It was spring break. We live close to the train station, so I walked home. I remember the tulips and crocuses were out. I thought to myself, Mom's garden is really taking off for a change this year. She must be happy. I let myself in, but there was no one home. I went into the kitchen, and from the looks of things, Mom was fixing herself a cup of tea with lemon and honey, the way she did whenever I had a cold. I wondered if she was catching cold. Then I smelled something funny, like something was rotting. I followed the smell to the door that leads to the garage. The stench made me gag. I only got a glimpse of her body, then I slammed the door shut and called the police."

Angela was quiet for a few minutes, then picked up where she'd left off. "I wasn't supposed to see the police report, but I bribed a reporter who stole a copy for me. Do you know what that monster did to my mother? The next-door neighbor, this old retired guy, has a big garden and a lot of fancy machines. He's got this thing called a thatcher. It has about three hundred metal rods that whip into the ground to aerate it. Faraday stole the neighbor's thatcher and his Rototiller. That fucking monster tied up my mother, then ran her over with the Rototiller and the thatcher, one after the other, again and again and again. . . . She was just thirty-eight years old—she was beautiful . . ."

By then Sullivan had guided the Land Cruiser around to the back of the motel. The girl certainly had reason to hate; there was nothing he could say that would make it any better for her. He turned to her and saw the tears shimmering in her eyes. "Did they hurt you? The *federales*, I mean," he asked softly.

Angela shrugged. "They slapped me around some. No bruises, though. I understand Spanish. They were planning to rape me before they took me to Faraday's father."

Sullivan nodded, pressing his lips together. The corrupt *federales* got just what they deserved. "Come on, let's go in."

They went into the motel through the back door. It was still siesta time, so there was no one around. The cool dim hallway of the first floor was a welcome relief from the heat outside. Angela led the way to her room at the end of the hall.

The door was unlocked; furniture and clothes were strewn everywhere. She'd obviously put up quite a fight. Sullivan closed the door behind them. Despite the mess, the room was cool and inviting—pink stucco walls, ceiling fan, sheer curtains swaying in the breeze. Angela collapsed into a frayed green taffeta armchair, propping her chin on her hands. She was a lovely girl, really. A college girl training for the '88 Olympic team. A hurdler, Sullivan had discovered. Her lithe, athletic build aroused him. He liked women who were limber, muscular, and fierce.

She looked up at him, her hard eyes now soft and round. "I'm sorry if I messed up your operation, Sullivan. I got a little crazy waiting for news from down here. I had to see to it personally that Faraday got what he deserved. I felt I had to actively participate. Do you know what I mean?"

Sullivan nodded. He knew better than anyone how the need for vengeance affected people.

"We better do something about getting the rest of those cuffs off," he said, pointing to her wrists. "They must keep some tools in the cellar. I'll be right back—"

"No, don't go," she stopped him. "I kinda like them. Sort of kinky. I could start a new fashion trend." As she admired her new "bracelets," Sullivan noticed her eyes shifting again. Suddenly she was a catlike predator.

"You'll never get through customs with those things on your wrists."

"You're not going to make me go back to the States

so soon, are you?" she purred, standing up and entwining her arms around his massive neck.

"That's the plan."

She started to run her fingers through his thick chest hair, kneading the taut muscles that corded his body. "You can always change your plans." She reached down and grabbed his crotch, feeling his balls through his pants. There was more there than she could put in her palm, but then again, she wasn't thinking of putting it in her hand.

She unbuttoned her shirt and offered her breasts to him, firm and supple, pertly turned up at the nipples. She stripped before him, tempting him with her body, her eyes, her mouth. She ran her tongue over her upper lip as she stirred the downy mound between her legs with her slender fingers.

Sullivan's heavy artillery began to throb. She was beautiful, the perfect body. Jane Fonda had nothing on Angela, and Sullivan was eager to do the workout. He paused and thought of his mission. The last *federal* never made it to a phone, so Faraday had no idea where he was. The Land Cruiser out back could give them away, but if there was no one looking for him, he'd have time to ditch it. He had some time to spare.

He cupped his hand on her hip and guided her to the bed. She fell back against the sheets, biting her lower lip, still fondling herself, waiting for him to join her. By the time he was undressed, she was ready for him.

They wrestled on the bed for a while, each trying to devour the other's hot mouth. She insisted on being on top, impaling herself on Sullivan. She rode him hard, and he was a relentless mechanical bull under her.

"I'm not gonna come," she hissed, taunting him.

"Suit yourself," he said, flipping her over and sinking into her from behind, doggy-style. He worked her slowly but strongly, and she squealed with each thrust. But still she refused to come. It was her challenge to his *machismo*.

He picked up the pace, thrusting harder and faster. She shuddered and strained, on the verge of climax. Then with a scream of agony she wrenched herself from him.

She turned and sat before him, and in one motion she gripped his lean butt and pulled his shaft into her mouth, working it like a giant candy cane. Her tongue swirled around as she pumped in and out, determined to make him come first.

Sullivan gritted his teeth, beginning to get light-headed with desire. He tried to push her off him, but she would not let go. He finally managed to separate her mouth from his engorged member and threw her back against the pillows. He pinned her shoulders down and entered her in the missionary position.

Angela screamed and fought him, but he gave her long, slow strokes, driving her crazy with passion. She didn't want to succumb to him, but he was overpowering. He thrust harder, digging deeper into her cleft. Then the explosions started within her. Small at first, like blasting caps on a fuel tank, then more intense, and she screamed and begged for him to stop and not stop.

When he was satisfied that he'd won, he let go, gushing all over her fires. After he was through, she sank into the sheets, worn and spent. . . .

Sullivan glanced at the window. It was twilight. They'd been at it for more than an hour. He reached over and picked up his bush jacket, searching for his pack of Lucky Strikes. When he found the pack, he stuck one in his mouth, then offered one to Angela.

"Fuck off!" she spat, slapping the pack out of his hand. Her eyes had that maniacal glint again, and in the diminishing light they looked like panther eyes. "You're all alike," she snarled. "First you rape me, then you want to be nice to me. Well, just . . . fuck off!"

"What the hell are you talking about?" Sullivan mumbled, lighting his cigarette.

"You know what I'm talking about!" She bolted up in

bed and glared at him. "You take advantage of me, then you make like it was nothing!" She balled her fist and pounded Sullivan's chest repeatedly until her hand hurt.

Sullivan had an urge to slap her back to her senses, but it was clear that she was disturbed. Her mother's murder had put her through hell, and she had good reason to hate all men. Now she was convinced that it was Sullivan who'd seduced *her*. In her present state, she couldn't deal with the thought that she had actually enjoyed her time with him. Now she was venting her pent-up anger on him, and he was willing to tolerate it so she could get it out of her system.

"Damn you ... goddamn you," she sobbed, trying desperately to hurt him. Finally she screamed in frustration, then broke down into uncontrollable tears. He sat up, and she immediately fled from the bed, retreating to the armchair by the window. Rocking back and forth with her knees tucked up to her chest, she cried, staring wide-eyed, like a scared cat stuck in a tree.

Sullivan got out of bed and started getting dressed. There was no time to hang around and coddle Angela. Besides, she didn't want his sympathy right now. He had to get rid of the police Land Cruiser fast—drive it off the cliff and let the jungle have it. And as long as Faraday didn't know that Angela was in Santa Celesta, he could use the motel as his base for a while. Angela was pretty wrung-out; he figured she'd stay put for the night.

"Listen," he said, "I've got a few things to take care of, but I'll be back."

She didn't answer and he hadn't expected her to.

He belted the kukri around his waist, then turned to go. Suddenly he stopped at the doorway. "I'm going to kill Faraday. You have to believe that. I made you and your group a promise, and I never renege on a promise."

She just kept rocking in the shadows. Sullivan left, more determined than ever.

16

Getting It Together

In the early-evening darkness, the limping Land Cruiser didn't look as suspicious as it had. Sullivan drove it back toward the center of town until the wheel rim cut the tire to shreds and started making a terrible racket. He decided it was time to ditch the vehicle, so he turned it toward the cliff, left it in gear with the motor idling, and jumped out. The engine chugged and strained, threatening to choke out, but it shuddered forward a few feet, then a few more. A loud clunk echoed through the night. The front wheels hung over the edge while the backs tottered off the ground, spinning in the air.

"Shit," Sullivan groaned. "Nothing works right in this country."

He grabbed the rear bumper and heaved, toppling the Land Cruiser over the edge. It tripped over the rocks and skidded down on its back. Sparks and the crunch of mangled metal silenced the jungle. Then the gas tank blew, casting an eerie orange glow over the black-green foliage for a few moments. When the Land Cruiser hit bottom, it was immediately consumed by the hungry jungle. The fire would burn itself out in twenty minutes or so, and the likelihood of anyone finding the truck in the near future was minuscule.

Maybe someday, years from now, someone would come across its rusted skeleton. It reminded Sullivan of the times he'd found MIA's while out on patrol in Vietnam, rotten skin stretched across their skulls, dog tags still fastened around their bony necks. The thought of being left to die in the jungle like that sent a shiver up his spine.

The next order of business was getting into town and retrieving his arsenal. Besides the kukri, he had only the *federal*'s pistol and just a half-dozen cartridges in the clip. He'd searched the Land Cruiser for extra ammo and come up empty. The thought of hiking the last mile into Santa Celesta on the road with little firepower didn't sit well with him, but under the circumstances, he had no choice.

Luckily, there was no moon tonight; he could sneak into town under cover of darkness. The gravel crunched under his boots as he strode down the hill, thinking back over everything that had happened in the past thirty-six hours. He'd infiltrated Faraday's fortress, found out that Faraday Senior was, in his own way, as bad as Faraday Junior and that the place was crawling with killers and perverts, eliminated at least half of those killers, and collected enough information about the layout of the *castillo* to begin planning a raid. But Sullivan still felt somehow that he'd been running in place, expending a lot of energy and getting nowhere. Preminger had betrayed him, and now Angela Mills was here to get in the way. Complications, always complications. . . .

As Sullivan approached the center of town, everything was quiet and deserted except for the cantina, where the lights from inside illuminated the porch and the sound of boisterous voices filtered out to the street. Sullivan looked for the old pickup truck he'd taken, the truck he'd left his olive-drab duffel in. He combed the square for a sign of the old truck, but it was gone, the CAWS automatic shotgun and the M79 grenade launcher with it.

"Shit," Sullivan growled, wondering how the hell he could do anything with just six bullets. Then he spotted Ramón's beer stand. There was an outline of light around the door frame. Sullivan decided to see if he could find out anything from the funny little man who'd helped him escape the *federales* that afternoon.

Sullivan knocked on the flimsy door.

"*Sí?*" Ramón sounded glum.

When Sullivan opened the door, he found the man sitting on a carton, his head propped on his hands.

"Ah, *señor*, come in, come in. But close the door behind you." Ramón rearranged a few cartons and gestured for Sullivan to sit.

"I'm glad to see you're still around, Ramón. I was afraid you might have taken the heat for the Mexican standoff."

"No, no, *señor*. The man who saw my face died, the other is still unconscious." Ramón sighed deeply.

"Then why so sad?"

"I am sad for Santa Celesta, *señor*." Ramón threw up his hands. "We are a town without honor."

"How do you mean?"

"Today, *señor*, is the feast of our patron saint, Santa Celesta. But where are the festivities? Where are the people paying their respects? Nowhere. Only the filthy *federales* and their whores celebrate tonight, just as they do every night in the cantina."

"Where are the rest of the people?"

"The rich man's money has polluted our lovely jungle. Those who work for him have too much money for tequila. They care nothing for tradition. And those who do not work for Señor Faraday are afraid to come out, afraid that Faraday's men will kill them just for the fun of it. It is disgusting, no?"

"Faraday's men have been going after innocent people?" The muscles in Sullivan's jaw bulged.

"Faraday's men do what they want. Do you know the leader of the killers, the fat man Ludlow? He came to town one day last week and for no reason he shot a dog in the middle of the street. A puppy, *señor,* that belonged to a little boy named Miguel. Just seven years old. He saw Ludlow shoot his dog and he cried and cried. Miguel followed Ludlow into the cantina and asked him why he did this horrible thing. The pig was drinking tequila with a woman and he did not wish to be bothered. He hit the boy hard with the back of his hand. Miguel, he fall back and hit his head on the floor. Now he is blind in one eye." Ramón shook his head in disgust. "Santa Celesta does not belong to us any longer, *señor.*"

Sullivan was so mad he could barely speak. "Yeah, but isn't having all these guys here good for your business?"

"Who cares about business when you have no freedom?" Ramón was shaking, he was so angry.

Sullivan nodded gravely. Ramón had hit the nail on the head. "Tell me something, Ramón. Why did you help me out this afternoon? How did you know I wasn't just another one of Faraday's goons?"

"That's what I thought at first, but when I overheard that man Preminger talking to one of the *Federales,* I figured the 'dangerous man' from the United States they spoke of had to be you. I had a feeling you were different when you *bought* a beer from me instead of just taking it as Faraday's men do."

"What else can you tell me about Faraday's band of thugs?"

"Ah, it is not a band, *señor.* It is a small army! Today he has hired more men and every *federal* in the area is already in his pocket. I hear he has thirty men at the *castillo* now." Ramón sighed again, despairing that Santa Celesta would ever be returned to his people.

"This is no time to be depressed, Ramón," Sullivan said with steely resignation in his voice. "Faraday and his merry men are going to go. You can count on it."

"But, *señor,* you are just one man. What can you do against all of them?"

"Don't worry about manpower. I'll take care of that.

The important thing now is that I find my weapons. I had a green duffel bag in this old pickup parked across from the police station. Any idea what happened to the truck or the bag?"

"The owner came for his truck, but the *federales* found your guns first. They took them to the police station."

"Then we have to go get them."

Ramón's eyes shot open in shock. "You are *loco, señor*. They will not give them back to you."

"Trust me, Ramón. Now, do you still have that Beretta you got from the *federal* today?"

Ramón reached down into an empty crate and came up with the automatic pistol. Sullivan checked it to see how many bullets he had. Nine. With his six, that made fifteen shots. Not great, but not bad.

"You can shoot, can't you, Ramón?"

"How should I know?" The little man shrugged. "My old gun never worked."

Sullivan looked at the ceiling. "All right, never mind. Just listen to me carefully and do as I say. . . ."

Inside the police station, two *federales* sat behind the front desk. The fat one with oily black slicked-back hair was dozing with his feet up on the desk, his fingers locked over his belly. The younger man was riveted to a porno comic book, his Dumbo ears casting large shadows across the pages. The chipped, scratched desk was littered with stray papers, coffee cups, and blunt pencils. The fat *federal*'s gunbelt lay on top of the clutter, the walnut grip of his weapon visible in the holster. The other *federal* was wearing his gun. They had settled in for a quiet night.

The sleeping *federal* snorted and twitched his nose. Flies buzzed around a pile of chicken bones in the wastepaper basket. The young *federal* flipped the page of his comic book and unconsciously started rubbing his crotch, his lips parted obscenely. Staring at the drawing of the nubile young heroine being whipped by the villainous stud, the *federal* began rubbing faster and harder, breathing heavily.

Suddenly the front door flew open and slammed against the wall. The young *federal*'s heart leapt as he dropped his hands and ditched the porno comic.

"Arrest this man! Right now! He is a thief!"

The fat *federal* awoke with a snort and instinctively reached for his pistol. When he realized what was going on, he relaxed and put back his weapon. It was only little Ramón dragging some dirty drunk in by his filthy peasant shirt.

"I demand that you arrest this pig!" Ramón yelled in Spanish.

"Stop your shouting," the fat *federal* ordered. He looked at the drunk stumbling over his own feet, hunched over like an old man, his grimy crushed fedora pulled down over his eyes. Disgusting, the cop thought.

"What is the problem? Explain," the young *federal* said with a great show of officiousness.

"He is a thief! He drank my beer and did not pay! Eleven cans of good beer! Fucking pig drunk." Ramón pounded Sullivan over the back for effect, and Sullivan shielded his head, continuing to stumble and weave, then falling across the desk, all the while scanning the room for his duffel bag. It was nowhere to be seen.

"Stop that!" the young *federal* barked. "We cannot help you. Get out, both of you."

The fat man snickered, bemused by the scene. "Go on, get out before we have to arrest you both."

"What do you mean?" Ramón shouted indignantly. "I am the victim of a crime, not the criminal. As a citizen of Santa Celesta, I demand justice. I demand that you do something!"

The greasy fat man wasn't amused anymore. He stood up, glaring at Ramón. Coming around the desk, he grabbed little Ramón by the shirtfront and pulled Ramón's face up to his own. "Now, you listen to me, Ramón. Do not tell us what to do. We do not serve the people

here. We serve Mr. Faraday. Your petty problems are
not our concern. Now, get out and take him with you."

Under the billowy shirt, Sullivan's chest heaved in
fury. Not only were these cops corrupt, they had the
gall to brag about it. These guys had no business being
in uniform, and Sullivan had every intention of taking
care of that.

He started to cough and retch, doubling over. The
federales yelled for him to get out before he threw up.
This was the signal. Ramón pulled his gun out from
under his shirt, stepping back a pace so that both *federales*
would be in his line of sight.

The cops were instantly silenced by the sight of unas-
suming little Ramón pointing a big gun at them. Then
the old drunk threw off his hat and stood up straight,
wielding a gun of his own. The *federales* were dumb-
founded by the almost supernatural transformation of
the stooped old drunk into a solid block of avenging
muscle.

"Where are my weapons?" he grunted in Spanish.
"The green bag, where is it?"

The young *federal* shrugged, his raised hand shaking.
The fat man jutted his lower lip defiantly. He gazed at
Ramón with contempt. How dare this little man, this
fool who sold beer in the town square, hold a gun up to
him? he thought. He inhaled abruptly and spit in
Ramón's face.

Ramón's eyes bulged, a blue vein popping in his
neck. He raised the Beretta and shot the man in his fat
belly.

Sullivan saw it before it actually happened. The fat
man fell forward on top of the desk, groping for his
gun. The younger man drew his gun and fired wild,
once at Ramón, once at Sullivan. Sullivan leapt back as
he fired, plugging the young one in the neck and chest.
Ramón fell to his knees, shoved his gun in the fat man's
face, and pulled the trigger twice. What was left of the
fat *federal*'s head sat on the desktop—bloody brains on
the half-shell.

"That wasn't part of the plan," Sullivan growled, racing around the desk to search for the duffel. "We're going to have company now."

Ramón scowled down at the dead men. "I am sorry, *señor*, but if a man does not defend his honor, he is nothing."

"Yeah, well, I can't argue with that."

Sullivan started looking through the small rooms that lined the long hallway behind the front desk. Each room was a cluttered office or a filthy cell. He tossed each one, ripping through closets and under beds to find his arsenal. Ramón went downstairs to the basement to look.

"Shit," Sullivan growled under his breath. He hated to think that the goons at Faraday's *castillo* had gotten hold of his weapons. It would be another goddamn complication that would set him back weeks.

He rushed into the fourth messy office and started tossing the room, half-convinced that his guns weren't in the police station at all. But when he got to the closet, a long grin spread across his face. There on the floor in a corner was his duffel.

Sullivan pulled it out and hunkered down to check if everything was there. The M79 grenade launcher was inside, but the CAWS automatic shotgun was missing.

Then he heard a familiar click behind him, the click of a safety being released.

He turned slowly. Standing in the doorway was a lean shirtless *federal* holding the CAWS at his hip, the muzzle leveled at Sullivan. The *federal*'s eyes had a deadly glitter, the sign of a man who doesn't hesitate to kill.

Before Sullivan could react, a shot broke the timeless silence, shattering the pall of death that had taken over the police station.

Blood gushed from a hole in the *federal*'s bare chest, a hole just to the left of dead center. His eyes glittered, but now they were like cut glass. After a prolonged moment, the man fell forward and crashed into a card-

board box full of office supplies. Standing in the doorway
was Ramón, the smoking Beretta in his hand.

"This is the second time you've saved my life today,
Ramón," Sullivan said wryly.

"Yes." Ramón nodded, visibly proud of himself. "I
know."

Sullivan picked up the shotgun and shoved it in his
duffel. "Well, let's not stick around and tempt fate. You
better get back to your booth. If anyone asks, tell them
you didn't see a thing. As far as anyone knows, you're
still innocent. Come on, let's go." Sullivan already had
one leg out the window, the duffel slung over his
shoulder.

"Wait, *señor*."

"What's wrong?"

"I do not want to be innocent. I want to help you rid
Santa Celesta of this evil." Ramón didn't look like a
funny little man anymore; he was proud, serious, and
ready.

"I'm counting on your help, Ramón. I need you here
in town to collect information for me. You've proven
yourself to be a worthy soldier. And when the time
comes, I'll make sure that everyone knows that you
were a big part of this operation. Believe it."

"Thank you, *señor*." Ramón followed Sullivan out the
window and into the darkness. He bade Sullivan fare-
well and slipped back to his booth.

Sullivan watched him disappear into the night. For
the very first time, he was beginning to feel good about
this mission. Ramón was a good man, a valuable asset, a
team player. Now all he needed was the rest of the
team and some careful planning and he could salvage
this operation.

Yeah . . . anything is possible, he thought as he
slipped into the shadows.

He had just one more thing to do tonight. At the
telegraph office.

17

Snakes and Demons

The next morning Sullivan woke up with the sun. He'd spent the night in a shed at the edge of a cornfield that bordered on the jungle. Getting up from his bed of dry corn husks, he saw the yellow-white sun coming up over Faraday's *castillo* far in the distance. Perched on the mountain, surrounded by a sea of green jungle, the fortress was like something from a fairy tale. It would have been a magnificent sight if Sullivan hadn't been aware of the perversion that dwelled behind those walls. It was a damn shame that the scum of the earth always gravitated to the most beautiful places.

Sullivan rubbed his shoulders for a little warmth. The night had been cold, but he didn't dare start a fire. Too many dry husks all around, and besides, a fire would have given his position away. He stood up and stamped his feet to get some feeling back in his toes. One leg had cramped in the cold, so he started to walk it off. When his "cramp" started to hiss, he took a closer look.

Coiled around his calf was a boa constrictor, an eight-footer by the looks of it. The snake was slowly barber-poling its way up Sullivan's leg, tightening its death grip as it traveled. A slender forked tongue darted out of a lipless green-gray mouth that seemed to be perma-nently frozen in a mocking grin.

"Oh, fuck," Sullivan groaned as the snake squeezed his knee. Quickly he reached for the kukri in his belt. He didn't notice the second boa in the rafters of the shed until it suddenly dropped to his shoulder and wrapped itself around his neck with the speed of a lasso.

The second snake wasted no time, flexing its body like a body builder's bicep. Sullivan gasped, his air supply cut off at the trachea. He clutched the viper with both hands, dropping the knife. He forgot about the pain in his leg.

He struggled to pull the snake off his neck, but it was as if the green diamond-back pattern were a part of his own flesh. The boa constricted again, and Sullivan fell to his knees. His head was light, and his stomach churned. Darkness was closing in around his vision. He was going to black out.

The boa around his neck relaxed slightly, then immediately put on the squeeze again. In that split-second Sullivan was able to get half a gulp of air, just enough to prevent suffocation for a few more seconds.

He gazed around him, desperately trying to collect his thoughts. Then he spotted his duffel on the dirt floor and remembered that he had a plastic bottle of animal repellent in it. One good douse in this bastard's ugly face, that's all it would take. If he could get to the duffel . . .

The snake squeezed again, and Sullivan's eyes glazed over. All he could see were shadows now. He lunged for the duffel, hoping he had the strength to get to it in time.

Of all the things Sullivan had done in his life, opening the zipper of that duffel and lifting the sixteen-ounce plastic bottle was by far the most strenuous thing he'd ever had to do. His face turned a sickening shade of blue, the color of the Blue Man's tattooed mug, as he struggled to control his fingers and unscrew the cap. Just one douse . . . one good spurt . . .

He finally managed to open the bottle but couldn't

locate the snake's goddamn head. He groped for it helplessly. With no feeling in his face, he couldn't tell where the snake began and ended. He collapsed on his face, clutching the bottle with both hands. Death was calling up to him from a deep black pit.

Then he saw it, its dead eyes looming over his right ear. Sullivan saw himself as well, as if through a dark mirror. He pointed the bottle toward the snake's head and squeezed with all the strength he had left.

The next thing he knew, the lights were coming back on and he was regaining his strength. The boa was gone from his neck. He looked down and saw his blurred reflection in the blade of the kukri.

A wrenching pain in his thigh yanked him back into full consciousness. The first snake was up to his thigh now, putting the death squeeze on Sullivan's entire leg. Sullivan groaned and winced, then quickly reached for the repellent. Suddenly he dropped the bottle and picked up the kukri instead.

He grabbed the snake around the neck just under its head. It unhinged its jaws, ready to swallow anything that got in its way. But Sullivan's blade was quicker. He sawed through the snake as if he were cutting through a hard salami. When the horrible head came away in his hand, he tossed it into the pile of corn husks. The coiled body immediately relaxed, and Sullivan unwound it from his leg like a heavy wrapping.

Struggling to his feet, he forced himself to walk in order to get the circulation flowing back into his legs. It was numb at first, then it ached like hell. It was going to be sore for a few days, but he didn't think there was any serious damage. He was pretty sure it wouldn't be an impediment to the mission.

The sun was up in the sky now. Sullivan had to get moving. Farmers would be arriving soon to tend their crops. He didn't want to be seen, especially by someone who'd go to Faraday to sell the information. He collected his duffel and hobbled out of the shed and into the jungle.

The early-morning jungle was cool and bright with shafts of white sunlight beaming down through the trees. It was pristine and beautiful in its mysterious way. Morning was the only time of day that the jungle wasn't dark and treacherous. That's what Lieutenant Simpson said every goddamn morning they were on that lurps mission to destroy that supposed munitions depot. Sullivan grinned to himself as he hacked his way through the Yucatán jungle, recalling his stock response to Simpson's daily wonderment at the green beauty that surrounded them every morning.

"Bullshit."

"You're a real hard-ass," Simpson would always say, laughing.

That was how they talked until the whole patrol nearly bought it at the trap munitions dump. After that, none of the men saw any good in anything. They were almost one hundred miles from the DMZ, deep in VC territory. One hundred miles of insidious, insect-ridden, death-trap jungle lay between them and safe turf. And to complicate matters, they'd had a wounded man, Floyd, who't taken a bullet in the leg. Floyd could walk with help, but they all knew it wouldn't be long before infection set in and the fever would start.

Morale had been as low as it could be. Even though they'd killed nearly three dozen Charlies in putting out the foo gas trap and the munitions-depot trap, they felt they'd failed. They hadn't gotten the big one they wanted, a real munitions depot. The hike back just seemed impossible, and Simpson didn't see anything beautiful about the jungle now.

The jungle seemed thicker and more oppressively hot, and consequently their pace had gotten slower by the day. Sullivan was practically carrying the whole patrol on his back, constantly encouraging, ordering, and coaxing them on. He tried not to show it, but he was worried. Jungle madness was not uncommon in Vietnam. Once a man thinks he's out too far, hopelessly cut off from his base camp, he begins to go crazy.

War is just a series of lifelines. All soldiers memorize the course that brought them to the jungle. Lurps soldiers knew that better than anyone. They all agreed that whenever they were out on a mission in the middle of some godforsaken stretch of jungle, all that ran through their minds was the way back to base camp, back to Saigon, back to the airport, and finally back home. It was an unspoken fact that at least ten percent of the reported MIA's were men who went nuts in the jungle and wandered off on their own, trying to find the way back home.

Simpson, Rainey, O'Keefe, Dodd, Mancini, Blake—none of them said what was on his mind, but Floyd in his feverish delirium cryptically spoke for them all. ". . . Lincoln, then Johnson, then Grant, then Hayes, then Garfield, then Arthur, then . . ." No one could figure out what he was muttering about. Finally Simpson figured it out. The streets in Floyd's home town were named after the presidents; in his mind, Floyd was walking home.

Sullivan knew then that he had to do something to pull his patrol back together. But all along, he knew there was only one thing that would help them, a big hit on an enemy target. Nothing succeeds like success, and if they were going to make it back, Sullivan knew they needed a victory. So when the opportunity came along, he jumped at it.

It was the fourth morning after the escape from the munitions-depot trap. Sullivan was bringing up the rear with the M60 machine gun poised in his arms when word was passed back from Simpson, who was on point. Charlie up ahead.

Sullivan rushed up to join Simpson and get a look for himself. Crouching in the brush, Sullivan took the field glasses from Simpson and focused on what at first looked like a disabled tank in the middle of the jungle.

"Is that what I think it is or what?" Simpson whispered.

Sullivan couldn't believe his eyes. It was a downed MIG-21 fighter jet. A patrol of nine VC were crawling

all over it like ants on a crust of bread. The jet was
demolished—both wings sheared off, tail missing—but
Charlie seemed very interested in the Russian-made
fighter. But what the hell was so interesting about a
wreck?

Then when two VC removed the cockpit canopy and
pulled out the lifeless body of the pilot, Sullivan got his
answer. The man's skin was sallow but his face wasn't
Asian. The pilot was definitely Caucasian—yellow hair,
overhanging brow, thick peasant features. There was
no doubt in Sullivan's mind that the pilot was a Russian. And when he got a good look at the unmistakable
face of the VC patrol commander, Sullivan's suspicions
were confirmed.

Phan Ky Zong, the Yellow Demon. Sullivan had read
so many intelligence reports about that gook he could
puke. Zong was ruthless, fearless, and maddeningly
evasive, the single most destructive guerrilla in the North
Vietnamese Army. He'd been credited with devastating
search-and-destroy missions on American positions deep
into South Vietnamese territory. He was responsible
for training the most deadly suicide troops since the
Japanese kamikaze pilots of World War II, men who
wouldn't think twice about carrying explosives into enemy villages and blowing themselves up along with
innocent women and children. Zong's most recent terrorist coup was the kidnapping of the wives of several
key Southern provincial governors, then demanding
that they swear their allegiance to the communist na-
tion of Ho Chi Minh. When he didn't get the replies he
wanted, he didn't ask twice. The women's heads were
returned to their husbands in the night. One governor
was said to have died of a heart attack when he got up
sleepily in the middle of the night to piss and found his
wife staring up at him from the bottom of the toilet
bowl.

There was no question in Sullivan's mind that that
was him. Just as the great Israeli general Moshe Dayan
was known for his eye patch, the Yellow Demon was

known for his skeletal face. His upper lip and most of his nose had been burned off in an explosion when he was a young man fighting the French. Nasal cartilage and teeth were permanently exposed, giving him a horrible death mask for a face. The mission had to be critical if the Yellow Demon was the commander.

It was widely known that the Soviets sold weapons to the North Vietnamese, but they always firmly denied that any of their troops were actively fighting with the Viet Cong. This pilot proved what the American military had suspected all along, that Russian troops were participating in the war. That's why Zong had been sent here—to get the Russian out before the South Vietnamese or the Americans did.

Simpson was practically drooling over the prospects of capturing the Russian's body. Sullivan thought of that as the appetizer. The Yellow Demon was going to be his main course.

When Sullivan informed his men of the target ahead, their lethargy was suddenly replaced by keen battle hunger. This was their chance to redeem themselves and salvage this mission. The munitions depot had been a bust, but a Russian pilot *and* the Yellow Demon was like hitting the lottery. Even Floyd pulled out of his delirium and turned into a battle machine, a little dented but deadly nonetheless.

Sullivan's plan was simple. Surround the enemy and attack on his signal. Just don't blow up the Russian.

The Yellow Demon's grating voice echoed through the area as he ordered his men to take whatever would burn from the MIG and build a fire. The savage wasn't even going to bother with trying to get the pilot's body back to his family. All he was concerned with was getting rid of the condemning evidence.

The VC guerrillas obediently stripped the fighter of whatever combustible materials they could find—tires and flight logs included—and piled them on top of a large dead branch they'd located nearby. The fire was reluctant to start in the moist jungle, but the Yellow

Demon screamed at his men to attend to it and make it burn. The Russian's body was laid out on the ground next to the pyre. As soon as the fire started to blaze, they'd throw him on top.

Eventually the flames started to climb; rancid black smoke hung over the wreckage. The agitated VC soldiers gibbered and yammered like baboons divvying up a carcass. Then Zong yelled for them to throw the body on the fire.

Two of the VC cheered as they went to pick up the body. But as they stooped for the Russian's arms and legs, machine-gun fire ripped through the smoky haze and the two VC toppled over, as dead as the Russian. The others started to return fire as they ran for cover behind the hulk of the MIG, but gunfire greeted them on the other side. They were surrounded and they had no clear idea where the enemy was. It was a straightforward ambush, Ho Chi Minh-style. Sullivan's men were delighted to give Charlie a taste of his own medicine.

Rainey, the sharpshooter of Sullivan's patrol, drew a bead on the space above the Russian's body. When two more VC lunged over the top of the MIG to roll the pilot onto the fire, Rainey picked them off like clay pigeons. The rest of Sullivan's patrol fired full-auto into the hull of the fighter, where the remaining VC had taken shelter. It was sweet revenge for Sullivan's men, giving these commies what their comrades had had in store for them at the munitions depot.

The VC were tough, though, returning fire sporadically as best they could from their cramped position in the MIG. Sullivan's men bore down harder; they weren't about to blow this mission.

But while his men were becoming confident of total victory, Sullivan was suspicious. The Yellow Demon was notorious for his ability to escape from certain doom. A guerrilla as experienced as Zong wouldn't jump into the fuselage of that dead MIG. That was like standing behind a paper target on a firing range. No, Zong was someplace else, making his escape.

Sullivan let up on the machine-gun fire for a moment and peered through the smoke, looking for Zong, hoping to outguess him. What would he do in Zong's position? Under attack, your men holed up in an impossible position, can't locate the enemy ... Maybe except for the flash of the M60 machine gun—

Instantly he realized that he was the only target visible to the enemy—then he felt the Demon's presence behind him. As he went to turn, yellow hands appeared before his eyes, ghostly yellow hands, and the glint of a commando knife. Sullivan dropped the M60 and snatched the wrist holding the knife intended for his throat. The Demon had Sullivan's left arm pinned behind his back, forcing him off balance. Sullivan battled to stay on his feet and keep the thirsty blade away from his flesh.

"Die, American, die!" the Demon commanded in a raspy whisper.

Zong was as strong as he was cagey and confident. He had done just what Sullivan would have done— sneaked around the perimeter to slit the throats of as many men as he could.

Sullivan fought to get leverage so he could flip the Demon, but he couldn't budge his attacker. Zong had the classic advantage of a short strong man over a tall strong man. Sullivan had to bend to Zong's height, which weakened any maneuver Sullivan had in mind. For the moment all Sullivan could do for himself was keep that blade from closing in any farther, and now it was less than six inches away from his Adam's apple.

"No way," Sullivan said through gritted teeth. "No way in hell."

But the knife kept coming, the Demon's hot breath hissing in his ear, the stained brown teeth laughing at Sullivan's defeat.

Then suddenly the explosion of a single gunshot rattled Sullivan's brain and jarred his kidneys. He thought he'd been shot ... until he realized that the knife had dropped from the limp yellow hand he was holding back. A dead weight slid off his back.

Sullivan turned to see the dead stare of the skull face lying on the ground. He looked up to see Floyd, the muzzle of his M16 poised over the Yellow Demon's heart. Floyd's eyes were clear and bright, all signs of jungle madness gone. As occasional cracks of diminished fire echoed in the background, Floyd and Sullivan exchanged the thumbs-up.

Sullivan would never forget the shit-eating grin on Floyd's face. There was nothing like having the support of good men, he thought as he hacked at another tangle of finger-thick overhanging vines.

The monotony of cutting a path through the Mexican jungle freed his mind to wander back to his lurps experiences in Nam. But now that he was finally coming up to the looming terra-cotta-colored cliffs, his thoughts returned to the present, to the Yucatán, to his mission, to his targets. Faraday's *castillo* sat atop that cliff like a gray-black wedding cake on a high pedestal. Sullivan stared up at the fortress, throbbing with anger. He was determined to get back into that place and kill the Faradays.

From the cover of the overhanging moss, Sullivan scanned the crenellated wall of the *castillo*. The turrets were empty, no sentries on duty. Faraday obviously expected the cliffs to repel an attack from the far side.

Sullivan examined the cliff carefully with a rock climber's eye, sizing up the possibilities, mentally plotting different routes. After ten minutes of studying the rocks, he decided on a zigzag route up a crack that led to a ledge protected by an overhanging lip. He'd have cover until the last forty feet. The last leg would have to be done after dark, which meant starting out at sunset. Sullivan nodded to himself. It was possible.

But not tonight. Not without support.

Just as he was about to pick up his field glasses and hike back through the jungle, Sullivan noticed a set of window shutters swinging open. It was a second-floor window. Sullivan raised the glasses to his eyes and focused on the figure standing at the window.

It was Jerome Junior. He was whittling away at the window frame with an eight-inch stiletto. His eyes were glassy and crazed. A silvery thread of drool hung from the corner of his lips to his shirtfront. Sullivan knew that look all too well. Faraday Junior had been cooped up too long. He needed to kill again. And if he escaped from his father's custody, no woman in the world would be safe, anywhere.

Jerome Faraday had to die . . . and soon.

18
Ambushed

It was siesta time when Sullivan returned to Ortega's Motel. After scouting out the jungle and the cliff under the *castillo*, he bummed a ride back to the motel from two American tourists looking for adventure in the Yucatán. The tourists—a young couple from New Jersey—were glad to give a fellow traveler a lift in their rented Ford Fiesta. After all, standing by the side of the road with his duffel over his shoulder, Sullivan did resemble a backpacker. But once he squeezed his incredible bulk into the minuscule backseat of the Fiesta, and they got a closer look at his scarred face, the young lawyer and his dance-instructor wife wished they could rescind their offer.

Sullivan saw their discomfort and eased their fears with contrived chitchat, feeding them a horror story about the awful food and accommodations in Santa Celesta, hoping that they'd pass right by and take the road out of town, the road that passed the motel. They seemed unconvinced, though, and Sullivan worried that the scared lawyer might try something clever like driving straight to the police station.

Sullivan knew their type—middle-class liberals who had teak furniture and original prints on the living-room walls. Usually they drove Volvos and contributed to all the right causes, basically straight arrows who thought of themselves as tasteful, knowledgeable, and adventurous. He knew exactly how to keep them out of Santa Celesta.

"Hard to believe," he said matter-of-factly, "but way down here in the jungle, they've got a McDonald's and a K-Mart. Right in the middle of Santa Celesta."

It worked like a charm. They'd do anything to avoid what they considered tacky, so they bypassed the sign for the *centro* and took Sullivan back to the motel, which he said he was checking out of immediately.

He entered the motel through the back door again just in case Faraday's men were onto him. Checking out the hallways and the lobby, he found them quiet and deserted, just as they should be at siesta time. Satisfied that there were no killers about, he headed for Angela's room, hoping that she'd come to her senses and just left for home. He didn't need her around getting in the way, and he sure didn't need any more of her neuroses. All he really needed now was some sleep.

But once he opened the louvered door and looked inside, he had a feeling he wasn't going to get much rest. Angela was still there, and from the dreamy look in her eye, Sullivan knew she had something else in mind for the bed.

"I waited up all night for you," she pouted. "Where were you?"

This was the kind of question that burned Sullivan's ass. He threw down his duffel and refused to answer.

"Don't be mad, Sullivan," she cooed, unbuttoning the top two buttons of her blouse and fanning her neck with a folded newspaper. "I just thought we had a good time yesterday, you know. I just thought . . ." She let her words trail off seductively like steam dissipating in the air.

He glared at her hotly. She had the most incredible body he'd ever seen, and he did want to have her again, despite the fact that she'd probably throw another fit afterward. His fatigue had passed, and now he was throbbing with energy. Still, he was wary of her. Angela Mills was definitely a complication, he reminded himself. Women always were.

"Well . . ." she sighed with great disappointment, "if you're too busy, I guess that's okay."

She turned toward the window and removed her blouse. Her jeans fell to the floor next. She reached back to unhook her bra, then turned around to face Sullivan as her luscious breasts spilled out. Their eyes locked, a small mischievous smile playing on her lips. Finally she stepped out of her panties and kicked them off. A mound of moist, soft turquoise cotton landed on the toe of Sullivan's scuffed size-twelve jungle boots.

"I'm going to take my siesta," she announced with a yawn.

"The hell you are," Sullivan mumbled, ripping off his bush jacket and throwing her over the armchair.

They devoured each other in a bruising kiss. He kneaded her breasts; she fought to unbuckle his belt.

"You can take your siesta later," he said, undoing the belt for himself.

Jerome Faraday Sr. was sitting in his high-backed leather desk chair facing the window when he heard a knock on the door. He ignored it, continuing to aim the Auto-Mag taken from Sullivan at the setting sun. He liked the gun; it gave him a heightened feeling of power and superiority. Faraday Senior liked to believe that he was powerful enough to shoot down the sun if he chose.

When the knocking at his door persisted, he scowled and whipped around in his swivel chair. "What?" he barked.

The carved mahogany door opened partway and Ludlow poked his head in. "I'm not disturbing you, Mr. Faraday, am I?" the obsequious fat man asked.

"Of course you're disturbing me, you sycophantic dirigible," Faraday shouted, the Auto-Mag gripped tightly in his fist.

Ludlow squinted at Faraday, trying to figure out what he'd just been called. Unable to determine whether he'd been insulted or not, he let it slide. "Mr. Faraday, we've got a little problem."

"Oh? How unique," the old man snapped sarcastically.

Ludlow opened the door all the way, and Faraday saw one of his *federales* holding a feisty peasant woman by the arm. The weathered brown woman, who could have been any age between twenty-five and sixty, squawked like a chicken, jabbering away in Spanish, clearly annoyed with Ludlow and the *federal*.

"Who is this woman?" Faraday demanded.

Ludlow cleared his throat and nervously eyed the long-muzzled gun in his boss's hand. "Well, Mr. Faraday, this old broad says she has to talk to you. She says she has some information you want, about Sullivan, but she won't tell us."

The woman screeched and waved from the doorway, trying to get Faraday's attention.

"Bring her in," Faraday said to the *federal*.

The woman's hungry eyes scoured the lavishly appointed office. Obviously she'd never seen such finery. Faraday was certain she was looking for something of value she could pocket. She approached the huge desk, bowing and scraping to the billionaire. Faraday recognized her behavior as simply a less subtle rendition of the way everybody else kowtowed to him.

"You"—Faraday pointed to the *federal*—"translate what she says."

The woman cooed like a whore to Faraday, gesturing and smiling as she jabbered.

"What does she want? As if I don't know."

"She says she knows where the man you want is. She says she will sell you the information for a modest price."

Faraday frowned. "How does she know what man I want?"

The *federal* asked the woman, then translated her answer. "She says she heard some other *federales* in

town describing the big man with the scarred face and
white streaks in his dark hair. She says she's seen him,
and that she knows for a fact where he is."

"How much?" Faraday sighed in exasperation. "What's
her price?"

The woman smiled like a Madonna as the *federal*
translated her price. "Ten thousand pesos, Señor
Faraday."

Faraday nodded and scratched the bridge of his nose
with the muzzle of the Auto-Mag. "All right, fine. Tell
her she has a deal, but first she must tell me where
Sullivan is hiding."

The overjoyed woman chattered away to the *federal*,
who then translated. "She says she works as a chamber-
maid at Ortega's Motel on the road out of Santa Celesta. She says Sullivan is staying at the motel with a
girl, a young American girl. They are together right
now in her room. Room seven."

An evil grin spread across Faraday's face. His knuck-
les were white around the pistol grip. "Good, very
good." He chuckled, standing up from his chair. "*Gracias,
señora.*"

As Faraday rounded his desk about to go, the woman
became agitated, angrily shrieking at the billionaire and
pointing to her palm.

"Oh, yes," Faraday said amiably, turning back to the
woman. "Your fee. I almost forgot." He smiled gra-
ciously and bowed at the waist to the little woman. "Mr.
Ludlow here will take care of you, *señora.*"

Then he looked to his henchmen, still smiling with
uncustomary friendliness. "Take the good woman upstairs to Jerome. He'll show her the time of her life."

Faraday's dry laughter echoed down the hall as he
rushed off to collect his men.

Sullivan reached over to the ashtray on the bed table
and snuffed out his cigarette, watching the last swirls of
smoke rise to the ceiling. He settled back into the
doubled-over pillow, feeling drowsy and relaxed. An-

gela was dozing next to him, her hand draped across his chest. He looked at her smooth, unlined face. She was soft as a kitten right now, but he couldn't help wondering if she'd wake up like a tiger again, lashing out at him, accusing him of seducing her.

He closed his eyes and decided not to worry about that now. Sex with her was terrific, even if she was a little hysterical afterward. Right now he just wanted to get a little rest . . . a little rest . . .

But the sound of gravel crunching under feet outside wouldn't let him rest. It was a sound he knew all too well. It wasn't a normal walk. It was the sound a man made when he was trying too hard to be quiet.

Sullivan's eyes shot open and he sat up in bed. Throwing off the sheets, he stepped into his pants, then went to the window and peered through the venetian blinds. Three of Faraday's thugs and two *federales* were taking up positions in the front parking lot. No doubt there were more out back.

"What's wrong?" Angela said, bolting up in bed.

"Trouble. Uninvited guests."

Sullivan crouched down to his duffel and reached for the grenade launcher, then changed his mind and took the CAWS automatic shotgun. The enemy were spread out all around him. His only chance of surviving this was to pick them off one by one.

"Will you tell me what's going on?" Angela said testily.

Sullivan ignored her, rushing over to the door. He opened it a crack, and instantly automatic fire chewed into the edge of the hall door. Shit, he thought, they've already covered the hallway.

Angela, wearing only her panties and a tight-fitting sleeveless T-shirt, ran to the bureau and took the Beretta 92SB.

"What're you going to do with that?" Sullivan growled sarcastically. "Curl your hair?"

"I can shoot," she replied, slapping a fresh clip into the gun.

"Fine. Get in the bathroom. When things get rolling,

you knock out the window and start shooting. But not before. Got it?"

She didn't have long to wait. Before she could retort with a smart answer, gunfire exploded through the room, riddling the splintered door. Angela ducked into the bathroom as Sullivan hit the floor. He aimed the shotgun and fired. The return fire ceased. There was a ragged, smoldering pothole in the door.

"That ought to make whoever else is out there stop and think," Sullivan muttered.

The window shattered with fire from outside, and glass shards rained down on Sullivan's back. He crawled away from the window, then crouched down beside the sill. Another blast of automatic fire ripped through the room, this time knocking the blinds across the room.

I wish I had an M60 right now, he thought to himself.

"Give it up, Sullivan. We've got you surrounded."

Sullivan squinted to see where the voice was coming from. Ludlow, holding a bullhorn, was crouched behind the fender of a *federal* Land Cruiser.

"Any way you slice it, you're dead, Sullivan." Ludlow snickered. "Give yourself up and the girl won't get hurt! Guaranteed!"

Sullivan saw red. What kind of a fool did Ludlow take him for?

"Who are you kidding, Fats? You'll save the girl for Jerome Junior."

"Are these the men who are protecting Faraday?" Angela screamed from the bathroom.

"Yup," Sullivan replied.

The next thing he heard was the crash of the bathroom window shattering, then the Beretta talking. He looked out to see Ludlow fall on his fat belly as Angela plugged holes in the Land Cruiser.

"I guess she *can* shoot," he mumbled to himself.

"Okay, fine. Fuck you both," Ludlow yelled into the bullhorn. "Everybody open fire! Let them have it!"

Sullivan got off two wild shots before Faraday's men opened up on the room. Sullivan hit the floor then, yelling for Angela to flatten into the tub for protection. Pieces of broken plaster, splinters, glass shards, and tufts of fabric flew through the room as if a cyclone had hit.

"Stay down," he yelled to Angela, wondering if she was still alive to hear him.

All he could do now was level the shotgun at the door. When the shooting stopped, Faraday's men would burst in, blasting to finish them off. If he survived the onslaught from outside, Sullivan would make damn sure no one came through the door. "Remember the Alamo," Sullivan muttered.

19

Getting Even

"Angela! You all right?" Sullivan yelled when there was a lull in the gunfire. He crawled on his belly to the bathroom door to see if she was still alive.

Her pretty head, now white with plaster dust, emerged from the chipped side of the tub. "Yeah," she said shakily. "I think so."

"Just stay down. There's more to come."

He crawled back to the window and peered out. Eight men with automatic rifles were reloading, just standing out in the open now as if they were taking target practice. Sullivan quickly raised the CAWS, aimed, and fired. The thug named Sal who'd almost nailed him back in Jerome's suite went down on his ass. Blood oozed over the gravel from a ragged five-inch hole in his gut.

One down, but the others started shooting again, and Sullivan had to duck. The adobe walls of the motel were thin and they didn't absorb bullets very well. Sullivan was afraid that it wouldn't be long before this little protection collapsed.

Plans and countermeasures played through his mind, but nothing seemed viable. They were trapped, plain and simple, and under the circumstances he couldn't think of a single risk, not one long-shot gamble, that might save them.

All of a sudden he thought of his old friend Malta, who'd met his end in an Oregon motel room with a woman. God damn, he thought, pondering the irony that he would go the same way his closest companion did.

"Hey, what's going on out there?" Angela yelled from the tub.

"Huh?" Thoughts of Malta had distracted Sullivan. Until now, he hadn't thought about the fact that although there was a lot of gunfire outside, none of it was coming into the room. There was shouting too, someone yelling like a cowboy on a cattle drive.

He went to the window, and smiled grimly. He'd wished for an M60 machine gun, and he got that and more. The "cowboy" was riding roughshod, hanging onto the roll bar of a charging Army-surplus Jeep while spraying Faraday's men with automatic fire, driving them off like cattle. The gunner was Johnny Merlin, Sullivan's old Vietnam buddy; behind the wheel was Merlin's merc partner, Bruno Rolff. They'd obviously received Sullivan's cable and had flown right down.

"Come on, we're checking out," Sullivan shouted, grabbing his duffel.

Angela didn't object. She rushed out of the bathroom, grabbed some clothes, and followed Sullivan out onto the balcony.

"Yo, Rolff!" Sullivan shouted, waving to the West German, who immediately threw the Jeep into reverse and backed up to the balcony.

Sullivan and Angela jumped down into the back of the Jeep behind Merlin.

"Sullivan! How the fuck you doing, man?" Merlin shouted with a crazy laugh while he continued to fire at Faraday's men.

"I'm a lot better than I was five minutes ago," Sullivan grunted, raising the CAWS to hold off the thugs who were coming around from the back. "Drive!" he yelled to Rolff.

The jerk of the Jeep tearing off threw Angela to the floor, but this time she didn't have to be told to stay put. The low-rumbling blasts of the automatic shotgun provided a bass line for the staccato rat-a-tat-tat of Merlin's machine gun and the rising whine of the Jeep's engine. Running for the jungle, Sullivan's team was back together again, making some heavy-duty rock-'n'-roll.

Sullivan took them to the stretch of jungle he'd scouted out that morning, the stretch that led to the cliffs where Faraday's *castillo* was perched. They took the Jeep in as far as they could go, then continued on foot until they came to a small clearing where they could set up camp. The four dropped their gear and sat down to take a breather. It was the first chance they'd had to rest since the rescue back at the motel.

Angela was a little fidgety around the men, though. These guys hardly said a word to one another, yet they seemed so close, almost supernaturally bonded. It was the kind of trust and comradeship shared only by men who've been to war together. It was something a woman couldn't understand.

"Well," she announced nervously, "you guys have already seen me in my underwear. I guess it's time we get formally introduced."

Rolff stared at her with his tiny ice-chip eyes, looking at her as if she were some kind of weird bug that'd crawled out from under a bush.

Sullivan regarded her with tolerance, making it clear that even though she'd proved that she could shoot a gun, she was still a hindrance to their mission. "Right. Well . . . this is Bruno Rolff. A bush-kill specialist . . . among other things."

She nodded to the solidly built man, trying not to stare at his shaved head and the Heidelberg scar on his cheek. His fatigues were still crisp despite the strenuous escape, and he hardly seemed to sweat. Rolff looked like an efficient machine of destruction, practical and deadly.

"And this," Sullivan continued, "is Johnny Merlin. An explosives expert, and a pretty good sniper."

"Fuck you, Sullivan. A *great* sniper," Merlin corrected. "How's it hanging?" he said to Angela as he pulled back his shoulder-length hair and tied it samurai-style.

"Hi ..." She forced a smile and tried to hide her dismay with Merlin's appearance. He wore threadbare jeans and a black T-shirt that proclaimed "Mercenaries don't die ... they just go to hell to regroup." His hair was long and his goatee was intentionally satanic. She'd noticed that he just couldn't sit still—if his knee wasn't bouncing, he was tapping his foot or doodling or playing with something. At the moment, he was clicking the safety on his M60 on and off, on and off. Johnny Merlin was her image of the kind of scum who was protecting Jerome Faraday. Thinking of him as a good guy would take some getting used to.

"Okay, listen up," Sullivan announced. "This is the drill."

Merlin and Rolff hunkered down by Sullivan's side and listened attentively, like the faithful listening to their guru.

"The target is that fortress over there." Sullivan pointed to the *castillo* in the distance. "Now, you brought the walkie-talkies I asked for, didn't you?"

Rolff nodded curtly.

"Good. You two will assault the front gates. Take the M79 and blow them open. Make a lot of noise, like you're going to bull your way in. That's when you'll call me on the walkie-talkie. I'll be around back, scaling the cliff."

Angela looked back at the cliff. Was he out of his mind? But she didn't question Sullivan's plan when she saw the other two nodding calmly, as if he told them he would be walking across the street.

"How many men are there in the fortress?" Rolff asked.

"There are supposed to be about twenty-five, but Faraday is a paranoid bastard and money is no object with him. I suspect he's hired more in the past few days."

"Maybe we should even out the odds a little bit before the big push," Merlin suggested.

"I'm way ahead of you," Sullivan grinned. "Special Forces ambush . . . Nam style."

Rolff's laugh was like a giant boulder rolling down a mountainside, quiet and low at first, building up to a loud, threatening rumble. Merlin whooped for joy. He hadn't felt at ease since he left Saigon. To Merlin, the thought of a jungle ambush was like going home for Thanksgiving dinner.

"I'll set it up tonight and join you before dawn. If I know Faraday, the fun should start just after sunup."

Angela shook her head in puzzlement. The three soldiers seemed to be in a great mood as they went to work unpacking their gear and setting up camp. Battle preparation was a pleasure some women just couldn't understand.

It was after two in the morning when Sullivan stalked around the back of the cantina and climbed through the storeroom window. The cantina had been closed for an hour, and no one lingered now.

Except for one, Sullivan hoped.

He closed the shutters and switched on the lamp on the table. The stacked boxes looked the same as when he'd left them. Sullivan pushed cardboard boxes off the wooden crate, then yanked the lid off.

The stench of Capitan Torres's rotting body made him wince. He pushed the packing hay away and prodded Preminger. When he heard a faint moan, Sullivan smiled.

"You're tougher than I thought, Preminger," Sullivan said as he hauled the man out of the crate.

Preminger coughed through his gag, gasping for fresh air. He blinked furiously, his eyes adjusting to light for the first time in over thirty hours. Sullivan dragged him over to a chair, hauling him by his ropes like a package.

Sullivan pulled up a chair, unsheathed his kukri, and stuck it into the table between them. Preminger sat there wild-eyed as Sullivan waited for his knife to stop vibrating before he continued.

"I'm going to give you a chance to redeem yourself, Preminger. I never give traitors a second chance, but in your case, I'm going to make an exception. Now, remember, this is a one-time offer. You blow it and you die. *Comprende?*"

Preminger nodded.

"Fine. Now, we are going to go into the cantina and you're going to call Mr. Faraday. You're going to tell him that you've been very busy tracking me in the jungle—that's why you haven't called in until now. Tell him you know where I am, that I'm holed up just off the path to the *castillo* with the girl and two other guys, about a half-mile from the main road. Tell Faraday that I'm wounded and that one of the other men took a bullet in the chest and is just hanging in there. You got all that?"

Preminger nodded.

Sullivan snatched up the kukri and dragged Preminger into the darkened cantina. Locating the phone behind the bar, Sullivan sat Preminger down on a stool and started to cut his ropes.

"Now, don't get cute, Preminger. Play it straight and you'll live to receive Social Security—not that you deserve it."

Preminger spit out the crumpled plastic from his mouth, coughing and wheezing. "A drink . . . I need a drink," he rasped.

"Later. First you make the call."

Sullivan slid the old black rotary phone in front of Preminger, who cast a sidelong glance at the gleaming kukri before he picked up the hook. Sullivan watched him like a hawk as he reached into his pocket for the slip of paper with Faraday Senior's phone number on it.

"This won't work, Sullivan—"

"Just do it," Sullivan snarled.

Preminger shook his head and started to dial. He held the phone to his ear for almost a minute before Faraday answered.

"Mr. Faraday? This is Preminger. . . . Yes, I know what time it is. . . . Yes, yes, I know I was supposed to call this afternoon, but if you'll just hear me out . . . No, Mr. Faraday, I was tracking Sullivan. I know where he is. Yes, I know where he is, and he's been wounded . . ."

Preminger proceeded to feed Faraday the misinformation just as Sullivan had laid it out for him.

"Right. Of course, Mr. Faraday. I'll be there." Preminger hung up the phone.

Sullivan slapped the flat of his kukri against his palm. "What did he say?"

"Don't worry, he bought it," Preminger moaned, rubbing his temples. "He's going to send his low-lifes out to find you at dawn. He told me to meet them on the path in case they can't find you."

"Good."

"Now, how about that drink?" Preminger groaned.

"Help yourself." Sullivan nodded to the bar.

Preminger leaned over to get something from under the bar. What Sullivan didn't know was that Preminger was reaching for the machete he had seen the bartender store there. Preminger came up with a bottle of beer in his left hand, and the machete in his right.

Sullivan had time to catch a glimpse of the long blade swooshing over his head. Instinctively he pushed back and fell off his stool.

Preminger stood up and squared off with the machete clutched in both hands like a samurai sword. He was weak, but he was angry, and that made him dangerous. But when Sullivan stood up to his full height with the hooked blade poised over his head like a lethal claw, Preminger's knees started to shake.

"You know something, Preminger? I knew there was a good reason why I never give traitors a second chance. Because no matter how fair you are with them, they end up stabbing you in the back anyway. I gave you a chance to live, Preminger, and you blew it. Now I'm going to have to put you back in the box with your friend. Permanently."

Sullivan stepped forward slowly, slowly . . . then in the dim light of the darkened cantina his blade struck like lightning.

The world was chalk-gray, and everything was still—the trees, the vines, the leaves, everything but the ever-present insects that treated them like breakfast treats. Angela was going crazy, wishing she could slap at the mosquitoes and scratch her bites, but Sullivan had told her not to move in any way. When she scratched a bite against his orders, he told her again, and in no uncertain terms. She listened this time. Merlin had tipped her off, and she knew that when the long scar across Sullivan's cheek turned white, it was no time to question orders.

Angela didn't exactly understand why they had to be so quiet and so still. The principles of guerrilla warfare were lost on her, but now she trusted Sullivan's battle wisdom. All night long, Merlin and Rolff had regaled her with stories of Sullivan's past missions. There was an air of bullshit about everything Merlin said, but when Rolff confirmed the tales, she had a feeling they were telling the truth. Still, she was amazed. She knew he was tough, but she never thought any one human being could be that tough.

When Sullivan reunited with them in the jungle just after five A.M., he immediately gave them the plan. Classic Vietnam Special Forces ambush. As he explained it to Angela, sit like a rock just off the trail until the

enemy patrol strolls into your range, then kill as many
as you can.

She was amazed that they were letting her take part
in the ambush, but as Rolff explained, "Another finger
on another trigger can't hurt." The West German bush-
kill specialist had given her a brief instruction in how to
use an AK-47 assault rifle to the best advantage, how to
aim for the head in order to hit the chest, how to stay
low and avoid return fire. Unfortunately she hadn't
been able to try out the unfamiliar weapon before the
ambush because that would have revealed their position. Now, with sweat pouring down her back in the
chill of the predawn jungle, Angela Mills was scared
shitless.

Sullivan had positioned them along the trail, drawing
on his Vietnam experience for the best results. Rolff
and Merlin were stationed on the left side of the path
about thirty yards apart, Rolff on the end closer to the
road, Merlin on the *castillo* side. Each man was equipped
with his own personal choice of weapon.

Rolff carried a Colt M16A2 Commando assault rifle,
a light, compact weapon suited for his role in the ambush. Any stragglers or deserters trying to get away to
the main road would have to contend with Rolff in the
bush. And in the bush, Rolff never missed.

Merlin's tried-and-true weapon was the tripod-
mounted 12.7mm M2HB heavy machine gun. What he
gave up in mobility, he more than made up for in
firepower. When Faraday's thugs tried to retreat to the
castillo, Merlin would be waiting for them with a big
surprise.

Sullivan was positioned on the right side of the path,
with Angela ten feet to his left. He would initiate the
ambush, using the M79 grenade launcher, taking out
as many men as he could while they were still clustered.
After the thugs scattered, he'd switch to the CAWS
automatic shotgun and clean up whoever was left.

Poised on one knee, the stout barrel of the M79

clutched in his hand, Sullivan was absolutely motion-less, waiting . . . waiting . . .

Long silvery rays beamed through the trees as the sun came over the horizon. In a matter of minutes, the jungle turned from gray to emerald green. Birds started chirping. Leafy branches swished overhead as the monkeys started their morning foraging for food. Blue-black bees the size of tennis balls buzzed down the path. Sullivan, Angela, Rolff, and Merlin didn't move. The jungle was beginning to heat up. They continued to wait.

Finally Sullivan heard it. Footsteps on the path, distant voices. In less than a minute he could make out what they were saying. Faraday's men were complaining about having to go out on patrol at dawn. As the first of the thugs passed Merlin's hidden position, Sullivan popped the safety on the grenade launcher and a humorless grin spread across his face.

As the thugs trudged down the trail, grumbling all the way, Sullivan began to recognize some familiar faces. Ludlow's right-hand men, Jake and Reece, were up front. Some of the *federales* who took part in the shoot-out at the motel were there, along with several new faces, Faraday's most recent employees no doubt. Bringing up the rear all by himself was K.C., the punk drug dealer. Sullivan counted twenty-three men.

He slowly raised the grenade launcher to his shoulder, waiting for K.C. to pass his position. Six grenades were arranged in front of him on the ground. K.C. finally stumbled past Sullivan's position.

Fantastic, Sullivan thought. They were all within range.

Four men were walking together just behind Jake and Reece, gabbing away, their weapons carelessly slung over their shoulders. Sullivan got them in his sights and slowly squeezed the trigger, relishing the first strike like a man warming up for foreplay.

A Fourth of July red flash sizzled out of the bush. The explosion shattered the morning calm of the jungle. Sullivan immediately reloaded, not stopping to savor the kill. He wanted to get off another shot before the thugs realized they were under attack. Finding another cluster of three, Sullivan aimed and fired without hesitation. Broken bodies flew through the smoke as the explosion severed the line of men.

Automatic fire ripped through the jungle, shredding vegetation and chewing up flesh. The thugs started to scramble, firing wild. Following Rolff's instructions, Angela aimed high, fired the AK-47, and downed one of the corrupt *federales*. Adrenaline gushed through her veins as she looked to Sullivan, feeling great. He gave her a wink and flashed that shit-eating grin his patrols were known for in Nam, then sent off another grenade. This was Sullivan's show now, and he liked it just fine.

20
A Real Cliff-hanger

The jungle was hazy with smoke and dust, and the shouts of the men under attack were drowned out by the nonstop gunfire. The rolling boom of Sullivan's shotgun thundered over the snare-drum racket of Merlin's machine gun. Only Angela could hear the faint strains of Merlin's scratchy voice singing a gleeful version of "Purple Haze."

The ambush was going down just the way Sullivan had predicted. He could personally account for eleven hits—seven men blown away with grenades, four blasted to kingdom come with the lethal CAWS. Angela had managed to bag two *federales*, and from the sounds of things up the trail, Merlin was doing a very good job of mowing down the retreating troops.

On the other end of the trail, Jake and Reece had taken off for the main road as soon as the first grenade went off behind them. They ran scared with shrapnel in their asses, abandoning ship.

"Shit, man, I'm through with this gig," Reece huffed as he hightailed it through the bush.

"I'm with you, buddy," Jake agreed, bounding ahead of his friend. "This Sullivan guy is out of our league."

They ran headlong, tripping over vines and raking

their faces on low branches. All they cared about now was getting the hell out of there.

But when the skull-headed German stepped out from behind a rubber tree, blocking their path, Jake lost control of his bladder and Reece nearly turned white.

"Halt!" Rolff barked.

The two thugs tried to raise their weapons, but Rolff's chattering Colt was faster. Jake's head split like a ripe melon; Reece's intestines burst through his bullet-riddled midsection and dribbled out his perforated shirt. Ludlow's right-hand men fell, a heap of steaming raw meat.

Suddenly all was quiet in the jungle, like the calm aftermath of a fatal car crash. Sullivan's men held their positions, waiting, listening. Angela's heart thumped like crazy—what the hell could happen next?

Sullivan stalked up next to her. "How many?" he whispered.

"What?"

"How many guys did you hit?"

"Uh, two, I guess."

"Don't guess. How many for sure?" he insisted.

"Two, definitely," she whispered, her hands shaking. "Two cops."

Sullivan nodded reassuringly. "Just stay down and be still until I tell you it's clear."

She nodded, unable to speak.

"Eleven and two," Sullivan shouted curtly.

"Seven," came echoing back from Merlin's position.

"*Zwei* . . . ah, two," Rolff called.

"That's only twenty-two," Sullivan hissed. "There's one more guy out there someplace." He scanned the jungle all around him, wondering where the hell the last thug was. There was no way he could have gotten away. Rolff was too thorough, and Merlin's machinegunning was merciless. The last guy had to be here someplace.

Sullivan slowly got up from his crouch and stalked forward, searching for the straggler. This went against the book; Merlin or Rolff could mistake him for the enemy and blow him away. But Sullivan had to risk it. He didn't want any survivors getting back to Faraday and reporting on Sullivan's true strength. He approached the trail, stepping cautiously.

"Drop the gun, Stark, Specialist, whatever the fuck your name is."

Sullivan followed the threatening Southern drawl up to a tree branch overhead where the muzzle of an AK-47 was poised less than ten feet from Sullivan's head. On the other end of that rifle, sitting on a horizontal branch, was K.C.

"Don't turn around," K.C. ordered. "Just drop the gun."

Sullivan had no choice. He let the CAWS slip to the ground.

"Okay, boy, now turn around real slow."

Sullivan reluctantly complied.

K.C. had a sick half-smile smeared across his face. He looked like a demented Cheshire cat. "You're pretty slick, I must say that." K.C. chuckled, then coughed. His shoulder was oozing blood. "But you're not as slick as ole K.C."

Sullivan just glared at the punk, wishing he could get his hands around the killer/drug-dealer's throat.

"I been hearing about you for days. Everybody up at the *castillo* fretting over what a tough som' bitch you're supposed to be, how you're the deadliest man God ever put on this earth, all that kinda shit. But looky who's got the big bad Specialist by the short hairs. Ole K.C., the guy everybody liked to pick on and make fun of. Well, no more. See, when I shoot down the Specialist, I'm gonna start getting me some respect up there. Matter of fact, I'm gonna take Ludlow's place as head honcho for Mr. Faraday."

"Who's going to believe you?" Sullivan sneered. "Old man Faraday certainly won't."

"Sure he will, he—" K.C. was interrupted by a coughing spasm. "He's gonna believe me sure as shit 'cause I'm gonna take that fancy knife of yours and cut your head off. I can just see Mr. Faraday's face when I plunk your head right down on his desk."

K.C. started coughing again. Then, when he finally composed himself, he raised the rifle to his shoulder. "This is a legendary moment." He laughed. "Just like when little Bobby Ford shot Jesse James. Now, kiss yer ass good-bye, Specialist."

A short burst of automatic fire shattered the tense calm of the jungle. The punk's body hit the ground, the whites of his dead eyes staring up at Sullivan. Standing under the tree was Rolff, a tendril of smoke snaking out of the muzzle of his Colt. He was looking casually up at the trees.

"Amazing what nasty things live in the trees down here," the mercenary said matter-of-factly.

"Amazing." Sullivan smiled.

Sullivan, Angela, Merlin, and Rolff had returned to base camp by noon, taking the opportunity to rest up before the big assault. After the ambush, they were all pumped up and ready to strike, but Sullivan knew it would be better to stick to the plan and wait till sundown. "But these guys are nothing," Merlin objected, hopping around like a flea. "We can take them before dinner, man."

"No, we stick to the plan," Sullivan insisted.

"But, Jack, I'm telling you we can finish them off easy—"

Sullivan turned on him abruptly and stopped Merlin with a hard stare. "Rememeber what we used to say in Nam? Get cocky and get killed. I made that mistake once down here and I nearly bought the farm for it. Faraday's men may be untrained, but they are all killers. And killers have a way of rising to the occasion for a bad cause."

Merlin didn't ask anymore.

But then there was Angela. Despite her good showing on the ambush, Sullivan wanted her out of the way for the big assault.

"I don't care what you say, Sullivan. I want to be there when you kill Faraday," she argued stubbornly. "Don't worry, I can take care of myself."

"No way." He stood firm. "You're staying right here at base camp."

He didn't tell her his real reason for not wanting her around the *castillo*. If they failed and Jerome Junior slipped through his fingers, he didn't want her anywhere nearby. The murderer of over 180 women was out of his mind now, like an animal that had been cooped up too long. He was dying to kill again, and he'd surely kill the first woman he came across.

Angela had a grating persistence about her, though, and she worked Sullivan all that afternoon. "I won't be satisfied unless I *see* him dead. My vengeance won't be complete, Sullivan. Don't you understand that?"

He did understand. Better than anyone else, he understood that burning need for full vengeance. That's why he relented and made a compromise with her.

"Okay, this is the deal. You go with Rolff and Johnny when we break camp at six. They'll set you up in a safe position near the front of the *castillo*. You will not take part in the attack. Do you understand that? When you hear that the shooting has stopped, you wait thirty minutes, then you can come in. But not before. Understand?"

"I understand," she agreed, sobered by Sullivan's grim tone. "I won't get in the way . . . promise."

At six P.M., they broke camp. Rolff and Merlin took Angela with them, beating the bush through the darkening jungle to take up their positions. Sullivan gathered up his weapons and checked his walkie-talkie, then made tracks for the trail he'd marked the day before, the trail to the cliff under Faraday's *castillo*.

As he left base, he looked through the foliage at the sun sitting low in the sky, like an orange balloon resting on the treetops. "It won't be long now," he muttered, then turned toward the *castillo* and headed for his target in double-time.

Merlin glanced at Rolff. Rolff shook his head slightly, his ice-blue eyes the only glimmer of light in the jungle now that the sun had gone down. They'd been partners so long they didn't have to talk to communicate anymore. Not yet, Rolff was telling his fidgety friend, not until we get the word from Sullivan.

Merlin stared at the walkie-talkie in Rolff's hand, waiting for it to speak. The small oblong box took on a life of its own in their minds—it was the gremlin who would light the fuse on the attack. Merlin wiped his sweaty palms on his pants, his eyes glued to the walkie-talkie. He refused to put the M79 grenade launcher down now. He wasn't going to miss a beat once Sullivan gave them the go-ahead.

At that very moment, Sullivan was hunkered down under the rocky overhang on the cliff, catching his breath after the climb up. There wasn't much left between him and his target, just thirty feet of difficult cliff. He controlled his breathing, calming himself, putting himself in the proper frame of mind for the battle ahead. He was bringing on the warrior trance that transformed him into a killing machine. Sullivan's mental preparations were similar to the way a pro linebacker psychs himself for a big game, or the moment of prayer the ancient samurai customarily performed before battle.

Finally Sullivan was ready, blood pumping through his veins like sparks firing a finely tuned engine. He detached the walkie-talkie from his belt.

"White King to White Bishop. Come in, White Bishop. Over."

"White Bishop to White King," Rolff's low voice returned. "Receiving, over."

"Is White Queen off the board and secure? Over."

"White Queen is off the board and out of the way. Over."

"Okay. You guys give me exactly five minutes. At

nineteen-twenty-three hours, make your move. Do you read, White Bishop?"

"Loud and clear, White King. Over and out."

Sullivan hooked the walkie-talkie back on his belt, slung the CAWS automatic shotgun over his shoulder, and stared up at the last leg of his climb. This was the tricky part. He'd considered alternative ways of getting up to the veranda, but nothing was viable. Hauling himself up over that overhang was the only way, and that was risky. Even though he'd wrapped rags around the metal grappling hook to reduce the clatter when he threw it up and attempted to hook it on the wrought-iron railing, Sullivan was gambling that there was no one up there. He wouldn't be able to see where he was going until he was over the lip, and sending the grappling hook up before him was like calling ahead to tell the enemy he was coming over.

"Well, here goes," he mumbled, swinging the hook over his head, gradually letting out rope. The hook sailed into the darkness above, the rope trailing behind it. It hit with a *thunk* that made Sullivan wince. Slowly he pulled down on the rope, fishing for something to grab hold of. He kept pulling until it wouldn't give. He put all his weight on the rope. It held.

Hand over hand, Sullivan hauled himself up the rope, his pumped-up biceps threatening to split the sleeves of his bush jacket. When he got to the over-hang, he locked his grip on the rope and swung his feet to the rock, getting into position to walk it. The CAWS on his back, the walkie-talkie and the sheathed kukri on his belt, and the 9mm. Beretta pistol that he hung around his neck on a length of rope, all dangled down behind him as his body became perpendicular with the rock face. Sullivan didn't want to think about the possibility that any one of those items might go careening down into the jungle below.

His face was contorted with the incredible effort he had to expend. He pulled and strained, careful not to take a misstep in the dark, praying there were no loose

rocks on this part of the cliff. The strain on his face
finally gave way to a grim grin of satisfaction as he
rounded the overhang. Now he was only hanging over
the edge at a forty-five degree angle. Don't look down,
and keep going, he ordered himself. Keep going.

"Hold it right there, Sullivan." The counterorder
came out of the dark like a command emerging from
the depths of his own consciousness. But the voice
wasn't his. He looked to the veranda, to the source of
that familiar wheezing grunt. It was Ludlow. The fat
man had a pistol leveled at Sullivan's chest and a commando knife poised over the taut rope.

"Oh, how sweet it is," Ludlow wheezed. "Revenge is
oh-so-sweet. Especially after you went to all the trouble
of giving me a choice of how I can kill you, you bastard."

Sullivan didn't bother to respond. He was too busy
trying to figure out his options. The Beretta was flat
against his chest now, but in his precarious position on
the edge of the rock, he couldn't let go of the rope to
draw. If he took another step to get his balance, Ludlow would start shooting. The fat man knew better with
Sullivan. Ludlow knew that if he gave him an inch,
Sullivan would take his life. No, Sullivan realized that
his only chance was a distraction, a good one. If Ludlow turned away when Rolff and Merlin blew the front
gates, Sullivan just might have a chance to get his
balance and get to his gun. But even then Sullivan had
to gamble that Ludlow's first shot would miss. And at
twelve feet away, that wasn't very likely.

Sullivan took a deep breath and prepared to be
wounded.

"For a legend, you sure are dumb, Sullivan. Soon as I
saw that hook flying out of the night, I knew you had
to be on the other end of it. You must take us for a
bunch of retards if you thought you could make it in
this way." Ludlow was having a great time insulting
Sullivan. That was fine with Sullivan, though. Ludlow
didn't realize he was helping Sullivan bide his time.

"Well, Mr. Specialist, don't you have anything to say

for yourself? As I remember, you used to be pretty quick with the smart remarks. Not so clever now, are you?" Ludlow then plucked the rope with the flat of his blade as if he were plucking a giant guitar string. "Shall I play you a tune?" The fat man roared with laughter.

"Do you take requests?" Sullivan muttered sarcastically.

"Go ahead and be cute." Ludlow scowled. "I'm gonna get the last laugh here, and you can count on that, pal."

The seconds dragged as Sullivan's awareness of the gun resting on his chest weighed on him like an anvil. He saw it happening in his mind, how he'd yank himself up to get his balance, while simultaneously grabbing the gun and firing. If only the goddamn blast would come.

Come on, come on, Sullivan mentally urged his buddies. You always were trigger-happy, Merlin. This is no fucking time to start showing restraint.

Then suddenly the sound of an explosion came crashing through the *castillo*, followed by a heavy rain of falling debris in the courtyard. It was Merlin's first grenade.

Sullivan started to make his move.

"Stop!" Ludlow yelled. The knife was still on the rope, the gun leveled in his outstretched hand. It didn't work! Ludlow wasn't distracted. But now he was mad. "You pig fucker," he growled. "You fucker," was all the fat man could say as he started to saw through the rope, his red eyes burning into Sullivan's skull.

"*White King, White King! Come in, White King!*"

"What the fuck?" Ludlow whipped his head around, looking for the source of the new voice.

It was the distraction Sullivan needed. He yanked the fraying rope and lunged for the wrought-iron rail just as his lifeline snapped. Clutching the railing with one hand, he grabbed the Beretta and fired.

Ludlow got off a shot that sparked off the railing and ricocheted into the night. Sullivan kept firing until the fat man fell. He leapt over the low railing and inspected Ludlow's mountain of quivering flesh, the stretched-tight polo shirt riddled with bloody polka dots across his immense belly.

"White King, come in, White King! Sullivan, are you all right?" Rolff's voice demanded.

Sullivan ripped the walkie-talkie from his belt and pressed the transmission button. "I'm fine now, White Bishop. Thanks to you."

"Listen, Sullivan. White Queen, the girl, she's inside."

"What?"

"The girl didn't stay where we put her. Once the gates fell, she made a run for the *castillo*. She's inside now."

"Stick with the plan, White Bishop. I'll worry about the fucking White Queen."

Sullivan stuck the Beretta in his waistband and whipped the CAWS off his shoulder. "Complications," he growled angrily. "Always complications."

He ran into the courtyard, scanning the ramparts for sentries. There were two at the corner turrets firing down on Rolff and Merlin. Sullivan raised the shotgun and sighted one of the snipers, quickly getting the man's chest in his cross hairs. The thunderous boom of the shotgun was still echoing off the *castillo* walls when the man hit the granite floor of the courtyard.

Sullivan aimed at the second sniper, but automatic fire ripped by his head and he was forced to hit the ground.

"Get him!" Old man Faraday's cronelike voice screamed through the courtyard. "Alive! I want him alive!" the old man shrieked in a frenzy.

Sullivan looked behind him and saw three thugs running his way, weapons trained on him. Faraday Senior was right behind them, screaming orders.

Sullivan immediately swung the shotgun around toward them, when—

"Sullivan!" A horrible scream for help was mercilessly choked off at the end. He turned to the plea.

At the top of the steps leading to the second floor, Angela Mills was being dragged from behind by Jerome Faraday Jr. He was yanking on a piano-wire garrote wrapped around her neck, forcing her up to his suite. The sick expression on Faraday's contorted face meant just one thing. The psycho killer was lusting to kill again.

"Ang—" But Sullivan's yell was cut short by a jack-boot in the ribs and the jab of a cold muzzle in his neck.

"Get him up!" Faraday Senior shrieked. "Take him to my office! Immediately!"

Sullivan stared into the old man's face as the thugs hauled him to his feet and took his weapons. He saw the same demented-killer expression he'd just seen on Jerome Junior.

21

The End of the Line

Faraday Senior marched ahead of them, leading the way back to his office. Sullivan followed reluctantly, urged on by three cold steel muzzles, two in his back, one at the base of his neck. Faraday's thugs weren't going to take any chances with him this time, having seen how dangerous the Specialist could be.

Merlin's grenade fire had already put out both front turrets, and from the sounds of things, he wasn't finished yet. Sullivan could hear the racket of the heavy machine gun as well. Rolff was keeping them busy out front. Sullivan wondered if these three were the only thugs left inside.

"This way, this way!" Faraday cawed. "Into my office!"

Faraday rushed to his desk and sat down in the high-backed leather chair. "On the sofa! Put him on the sofa!"

The thugs shoved Sullivan down onto the tufted maroon leather sofa, then fanned out around him, their weapons at the ready. Sullivan studied their faces— two of them were *federales* he hadn't seen before and the other was a broken-nosed thug he remembered from the mess hall.

"All right, the three of you, out!" Faraday ordered. "I'll take care of the Specialist."

Faraday was holding the .44 Auto-Mag he'd taken from Sullivan. Placed on the desk was the polished skull of his ex-partner, Mr. Williams. The long-barreled pistol in the old man's liver-spotted hands was like a cobra ready to strike.

When his men didn't move, Faraday became impatient. "I said get out!" he screamed. "Wait outside! Sullivan is mine!"

"But, Mr. Faraday," the broken-nosed thug objected, "this guy is too dangerous. We can't leave you alone with him."

"Are you deaf as well as stupid? I said get out!"

"But, Mr.—"

The Auto-Mag struck, spitting fire from its viper maw. The broken-nosed thug fell to the carpet, dead. The bullet had passed clean through his chest and lodged in the paneled wall.

"Now, do I have to say it again? Get out! Now!" Faraday fired into the ceiling. The two *federales* ran out into the hallway and slammed the door behind them. They didn't want to be told again.

Faraday cackled like a witch, his eyes wild and maniacal. He was as crazy as his son, Sullivan was certain of that now, but Faraday Senior wasn't careless. Sullivan noticed that with all his ranting and carrying on, the Auto-Mag remained rock-solid in his hand.

"What a presumptuous fool you are, Mr. Sullivan. To think that you could infiltrate my empire and strike at the heart of my family was utter folly. You're like a virus trying to infect the Faraday family, but I have news for you, Mr. Sullivan. The Faradays are strong; we can fend off invading bacteria like you."

"Your son is a mass murderer and a fugitive from justice," Sullivan growled. "He deserves to die."

"Why are you all so hard on my poor boy?" the old man complained. "Mr. Sullivan, I'm sure even you have been guilty of a little indiscretion sometime in your life."

"Murdering a hundred and eighty women is not a 'little indiscretion.' "

Faraday shook his head and looked up at the portrait of Sumner W. Faraday hanging on the wall opposite Sullivan. "They just don't understand us, Sumner. You had the same problem. So did Grandfather, and Father too. People just don't realize that we Faradays are different. Fate has chosen us to be rich and powerful for a reason. We aren't subject to the same laws and rules that govern petty men. We are above society's so-called 'justice.' Aren't we, Sumner?"

"Bullshit," Sullivan spat. "No one is above justice."

Faraday whipped his head around and glared at Sullivan. "Is that so?" He turned back to the portrait. "I've brought this impertinent subspecies here to you, Sumner, so that I can show you how I'm dealing with family affairs. I know you think I've failed you in many ways, that I've let family crises get out of hand, but that isn't so, Sumner. You'll see how ruthless I can be with an underling. Just as you were with your employees in South Africa, Sumner. I'll handle this just the way you would." Faraday pleaded pathetically for forgiveness from the lifeless portrait.

"Now, as for you, Mr. Sullivan . . ." Faraday's tone became imperiously arrogant again when he looked at Sullivan. The old man picked up the skull and weighed it in his hand. "Do you remember Mr. Williams?" Faraday tossed the skull to Sullivan, who caught it single-handedly. "You two should get acquainted, Mr. Sullivan. You and Mr. Williams will be meeting in the here-after very soon."

Faraday cackled demoniacally as Sullivan palmed the heavy skull in his huge hand. In high school Sullivan had been the ace relief pitcher on the varsity baseball team. He had only one pitch, an incredibly accurate fastball that was once clocked by an American League scout at 96 mph. Sullivan wondered if he still had his stuff.

Faraday turned to the portrait again. "Now, Sumner, I want you to watch how—"

The skull flew from Sullivan's hand, across the room, and struck Faraday's gun hand with enough force to crack bone. The gun tumbled to the blotter, and Sullivan lunged for the desk, pens, papers, and ledgers falling to the floor. Faraday snatched it up again, but Sullivan grabbed Faraday's hand holding the gun. Faraday struggled to get off a shot at Sullivan, but as he squeezed the trigger, Sullivan snapped the muzzle away from himself. And toward Faraday.

The bullet entered under Faraday's chin and exited through the top of his hairless head. Blood oozed over his forehead and dribbled down his face, dripping onto his immaculate white linen suit.

Disengaging the gun from Faraday's spidery fingers, Sullivan glanced up at the hard-eyed portrait on the wall. Sumner W. Faraday didn't seem to give a fuck about Jerome Senior.

The sound of automatic fire just outside the door sent Sullivan to the floor behind the desk. The door swung open and the lifeless body of one of the *federales* fell into the room. Sullivan aimed at the doorway, ready to shoot. Then Merlin appeared on the threshold, scanning the room with an AK-47 assault rifle on his hip.

"Hold your fire, Merlin."

Sullivan got to his feet.

"Where's the girl?" Merlin asked.

"Upstairs, follow me."

As they stepped over the bodies of the two dead *federales* and ran down the hall, the bark of Rolff's Colt echoed through the courtyard as he finished off two more of Faraday's thugs. There was only one man left, the object of this mission, Jerome Faraday Junior. Sullivan only hoped he wasn't too late to save Angela.

Sullivan and Merlin entered the courtyard with guns ready. Rolff spotted them and started to backstep through the courtyard, covering his buddies' position.

Sullivan bounded up the stairs to the second-floor wing, Merlin hot on his heels. Racing down that red-carpeted hallway, they heard the sound of glass breaking and twin screams.

Sullivan crashed the heavy carved door to Faraday Junior's suite at a run, shattering the door. The scene before Sullivan's eyes hit him harder than a bullet in the gut. Angela and a Mexican whore were side by side on the bed tied to each other at the elbows, wrists, and feet, then tied to the bedposts by their outside feet and wrists. Half-naked, their clothes ripped and torn, the women lay stretched out like the two wings of a butterfly.

Seated at his table was Faraday Junior, oblivious of the intrusion. He was methodically breaking liquor bottles, selecting the longest shards from each break and setting them aside. Angela and the whore each already had a piece of brown beer-bottle glass embedded in their thighs.

Sullivan gritted his teeth and raised the Auto-Mag to the drooling psycho killer's face.

"No!" Angela screamed. "Don't kill him! He's mine!"

Sullivan's mouth was a contorted line of anger and confusion. "What the hell do you mean, don't kill him?"

Merlin had cut the women loose by now, and Angela ran up to Sullivan and pushed his gun away from Faraday's head. "He's mind, Sullivan. Please. *I* have to kill him. For my mother. Don't you understand?"

Sullivan stared into her face. He did understand. She needed to have complete vengeance. Hiring him to kill Faraday wasn't good enough. She had to do it herself.

But while Sullivan deliberated, Faraday Junior started to come out of his trance. He stared up at Sullivan's face, then looked down at the littered tabletop. Under the layer of broken glass were the pictures Faraday cut out of porno magazines, the ones he drew over and mutilated. His eyes focused on a black-and-white photograph his father had given him. It was a picture of someone his father had told him to beware of, the picture of Sullivan that Preminger had taken. Jerome couldn't relate to it the way it was, he couldn't really hate that person, so he'd altered the photo so he could hate him. He'd drawn long hair, makeup, and a dress over the picture of Sullivan. Now he could really hate that person.

Jerome grinned and clutched the broken neck of a tequila bottle. He looked up at Sullivan's face and lunged.

"Heads up!" Merlin yelled.

Instinctively Sullivan smashed Faraday across the side of the head with the heavy Auto-Mag. The psycho crumpled to the floor, stunned by the blow. He glared down at the detestable slug, wanting so bad to pull the trigger and send him to hell.

But Angela's dark pleading eyes kept him from doing it. She was right. She should kill the man who'd killed her mother.

"Okay," he said, offering her the Auto-Mag. "Here."

Angela shook her head and pointed to the sheathed kukri on Sullivan's belt. "I want that."

The Mexican whore concurred, nodding hysterically in agreement, rushing up to Angela's side. She would not be denied her share of the vengeance.

Surveying the array of bottles on the table, Sullivan found one that was half-full of tequila. He held it up to the light and swirled the amber liquor, looking at the tiny curling agave worm at the bottom. Finally Sullivan unsheathed his knife and put it in Angela's hands. Her eyes sparkled at the gleam of the polished steel blade.

"Come on," he muttered to Merlin. "Let's go have a drink. This may take a while."

The two mercenaries left the room as the two women hovered over Faraday like hysterical birds of prey. Without saying a word, each knew exactly what the other had in mind.

Out in the hallway, Sullivan and Merlin met Rolff coming up the stairs.

"I've checked all the rooms on the ground floor," Rolff reported. "I think we got all of them."

"Just about," Sullivan said, unscrewing the cap on the tequila bottle and handing it to Merlin.

Merlin took a long, well-deserved swig, then passed the bottle to Rolff.

Rolff glugged down three fingers' worth. "Ahhh," he breathed with satisfaction as he gave the bottle back to Sullivan.

Sullivan put the bottle to his lips and tilted it straight up. He drank until the agave worm floated down through the liquor and lodged between his front teeth. Suddenly a high, bloodcurdling scream broke the after-battle calm. It was the scream of a man losing something precious. Sullivan bit down on the worm and smiled.

DON'T MISS . . .

The following is an exciting excerpt
from the next novel in
the *Specialist* series
from Signet:

THE SPECIALIST #10
The Beirut Retaliation

"Ladies and Gentlemen, we are making our final approach to Beirut International Airport now. Our expected time of arrival is approximately twenty-two minutes from now. We hope you enjoyed your flight, and on behalf of the entire crew I'd like to thank you for flying . . ."

Jack Sullivan turned the page of the *International Herald Tribune*, half-listening to the pilot's message. He wasn't paying much attention to the newspaper either. He was preoccupied with thoughts of Project Scalpel.

The first-class cabin gradually came to life as the passengers—mostly businessmen and women from England and America—started to pack up their briefcases and stretch their legs before the seat-belt sign lit up. Sullivan reached into his breast pocket and pulled out a pack of Kents. Absently, he stuck one in his mouth, lit it with his Bic lighter, took a long drag, and grimaced.

Not his brand. Traveling undercover meant changing all his trademarks, including his favorite brand of cigarette, Luckies.

Sullivan's passport identified him as Raymond Sargent of Bristow, Virginia. Although the name was an alias, the passport was genuine U.S. government issue, courtesy of the FBI. Everything had to be perfect for Project Scalpel.

Project Scalpel was the biggest vengeance mission Sullivan had ever undertaken. It was also the first time he'd had the official sponsorship of the U.S. Government. Special Operations, a top-secret branch of the Department of Defense specializing in retaliation against terrorists, had commissioned Sullivan to lead a hand-picked commando team to avenge the murderous terrorist attacks on the American embassy and the Marine outpost in Beirut.

Over 200 Marines had been killed when a terrorist fanatic drove a truck full of explosives into that Marine compound. They were all good men doing their best to serve their country. Since Sullivan considered all fighting men like family, this mission was a personal vendetta for him. He wanted bloody vengeance for the mass execution of his brothers and the insults America had suffered at the hands of ruthless terrorists in Lebanon.

But Sullivan's objective for the moment was to get into Lebanon undetected and rendezvous with his team. If his targets knew the Specialist was in Beirut, they'd scatter like cockroaches. That's why he was traveling as Raymond Sargent, a salesmen for Heckler & Koch going to Beirut to sell weapons to the Lebanese government. That's why he was smoking Kents instead of Luckies. That's why he had altered his appearance.

On the advice of an FBI disguise expert, Sullivan wore a loose-fitting drab brown suit to camouflage his six-four, 240-pound, bodybuilder physique. To cover the knife scar that bisected his left eyebrow, he wore yellow-tinted eyeglasses, which also obscured the intense gunmetal gray eyes that often resembled the steely gaze of a double-barreled shotgun. The long blue scar across his right cheek had been spackled with a long-wearing Latex compound. And the white streaks along his temples had been dyed black to match the rest of his close-cropped hair. The only feature they couldn't alter was his left ear, where a .38-caliber slug had ripped the lobe off.

The skinny man sitting next to Sullivan removed his Coke-bottle glasses and began to polish them carefully with a crumpled handkerchief. His name was Fitzwack, and he'd told Sullivan he was an engineer trying to sell a new system for cleaning up toxic waste dumps. Sullivan's first thought when he saw Fitzwack was that his long drooping nose was too big for his thin drawn face, and now, without his glasses, he looked like a beady-eyed anteater.

"I must admit, Ray," Fitzwack chuckled nervously, "the thought of being in Beirut makes me a little uneasy."

"It should," Sullivan grunted, then remembered to maintain his Raymond Sargent persona. "Well, what I mean by that, Fitz, is that selling in any Arab country is a real horror show. They're tough cookies when it comes to making big purchases in this part of the world. I'll tell you right now, it'll be trench warfare all the way."

Suddenly the curtain that separated the first-class section from tourist was ripped open. "Everyone will please give me their attention!"

A short wiry man wearing an ill-fitting suit without a tie stepped briskly up the aisle, flashing a Soviet-made PPD-40 submachine gun over the passengers' heads. The man had an almost cordial smile, but his dark-rimmed eyes were maniacal.

"This plane is being confiscated in the name of the Islamic People's Freedom Party," the hijacker announced. "We are going to Teheran. All American citizens will be held in our custody until the United States Government pays our party two million dollars in gold bullion and arranges for the release from Western prisons of the following political prisoners: Ali al-Halaq, Mehmet al . . .''

The hijacker continued his chant, reading the names of his terrorist buddies—the so-called "political prisoners" —from a list he'd pulled out of his pocket. Sullivan seethed. The success of Project Scalpel depended on timing. The schedule was tight enough as it was, and he needed every minute of the few days he had left for final training. He couldn't afford a little side trip to Iran. If he didn't get to Lebanon today, the whole mission could go down the drain. Besides, he hated hijackers, little men with big guns who threatened innocent people in the air. Everything about this new development pissed the hell out of Sullivan.

Complications, always complications, he thought angrily.

Sullivan's brain clicked like a computer, trying to come up with a viable plan. It was a very tricky situation. Firing weapons inside the plane while it was still in the air was very risky. If a stray bullet shattered a window they could all be killed by the change in compression. But even if he could use one, Sullivan had no gun. All he had on him were *pictures* of guns in his bogus sales portfolio.

He briefly considered lunging at the little fanatic and disarming him, but that was impractical. For one thing, the hijacker was probably trigger-happy and there were too many people crowded into the cabin. Sullivan also had no idea how many other hijackers were on the plane and on top of everything else, a heroic rescue attempt would blow his cover and put Project Scalpel in jeopardy. No, he had to think of something else.

"Jeez," Fitzwack mumbled to Sullivan, "another goddam hijacking! Somebody ought to do something."

Sullivan's eyes widened. Fitzwack just gave him an idea.

"Somebody ought to do something?" Sullivan said out loud so the hijacker could hear. "You're with the damn

CIA, right? So why don't *you* signal somebody. *Do something!*"

Fitzwack's receding chin dropped. "CIA? What are you talking about?"

The little fanatic heard them, just as Sullivan wanted, and the muzzle of his SMG was now trained on a point between Fitzwack's eyes.

"Get up," the hijacker ordered. "Both of you."

"But I'm a salesman," Sullivan sputtered.

"And I'm an engineer," Fitzwack protested.

"Yes, yes. Everyone in America is innocent," the hijacker laughed menacingly.

"But I'm telling you the truth," Fitzwack insisted. "I am innocent."

"You are American, and therefore you are the enemy! And if an Islamic court finds that you are CIA, then you will be executed. But first you will both make your full confessions over national Iranian radio once we reach Teheran. Ahmed!" he called out. "Ahmed, come quickly!"

A sad-eyed, unshaven face poked through the curtain that separated tourist from first class. "What is it?" the second hijacker shouted in Farsi.

"CIA!" the first hijacker pointed to Sullivan and Fitzwack. "Cover them. They are devils."

"But I must remain here with these infidels," Ahmed replied, clearly annoyed that their plan was being changed.

"Rashid and Yussan can handle the others. These are the real prizes. Did you take care of the one who smuggled the guns aboard?"

"Yes, I paid him well—with a quick death."

Sullivan knew a few words in the Iranian language, enough to figure out how the men had stowed their weapons. And he knew that he would have four hijackers to destroy.

"Come, CIA. Into the cockpit." Ahmed stuck the muzzle of his SMG into Sullivan's back, prodding him on.

"We must radio Teheran," the little fanatic crowed. "Tell them that we have very valuable hostages."

The hijacker kicked in the door to the cockpit and repeated his chant to the pilot and copilot, making sure they saw his gun. ". . . You will keep your eyes forward and you will not look back. If you disobey, you will die. Now, you will change course for Teheran."

The pilot turned to the little fanatic and shook his head. "We haven't got enough fuel to get to Teheran. We'll have to stop—"

The little fanatic smashed the butt of his gun down on the pilot's head. "Fool!" he screamed. "Allah will provide the fuel!"

Blood trickled from the pilot's scalp. Dazed and clutching his head, he turned back to the instrument panel and did as he was told.

The terrorist then turned to Sullivan and Fitzwack, eyeing them like lambs for the slaughter. "In what manner shall we extract confessions from these CIA, Ahmed?" he cackled.

Ahmed's expression was deadly serious. "Allah demands that they must suffer in accordance with their sins, as it is written."

But while the hijackers debated the exact manner of torture that would be appropriate for the "CIA men," Sullivan sized up the scene and very gradually positioned himself in the crowded space. He glanced to the closet behind Ahmed, then shifted his weight from one foot to the other, moving as he did so. The hijackers were standing face to face, Sullivan now off to the side but between them.

Sullivan took a deep breath, then made his move, attacking both hijackers simultaneously. A lightning karate chop with his left hand sent Ahmed's gun clattering to the floor. The other fanatic lifted his SMG to fire, but Sullivan grabbed the muzzle with his other hand and diverted the fire toward Ahmed. Slugs passed through Ahmed's chest and lodged harmlessly in the closet door, as Sullivan had planned.

Holding the terrorist's SMG up and away, Sullivan thrust a jackhammer knife hand into his midsection. The terrorist released his grip on the gun and doubled over in pain. Sullivan had to act fast. He forced the hijacker to the floor with his knee and held him down over the oozing corpse of his comrade. Firing at point-blank range, Sullivan sent the hijacker to his Maker, using Ahmed's body to catch the bullets that ripped through the little man's heart.

The sound of gunfire alerted Rashid and Yussan, but Sullivan had already anticipated their arrival. He was crouched to the side of the doorway when Rashid rushed into the cockpit. The PPD-40 in Sullivan's hands barked, spitting fire. The closet door took a half-dozen more bullet holes. Rashid fell onto the heap with his comrades. But the SMG's clip was empty.

Yussan, a grizzly one-eyed fanatic, flew into the cockpit waving an automatic pistol. He was poised to fire it when Sullivan, on his blind side, lunged. They wrestled on the floor, Sullivan smashing the man's gun hand with the butt of the SMG. Yussan kicked, screamed, struggled, even tried to bite Sullivan's arm, but he would not let go of the gun.

Suddenly, a heavy black wing-tip shoe stomped down on the man's hand. Sullivan glanced up to see a contorted grimace of fury on Fitzwack's bug-eyed face as he kicked the pistol into a corner.

Sullivan snapped the disarmed hijacker's arms to his sides, pinning them with his knees as he sat on the small of the man's back. Before Yussan could scream again, Sullivan locked his fingers under his chin and quickly yanked up, breaking the man's neck with a sharp crack. He died instantly.

"Holy shit!" Fitzwack breathed, swaying and pale after witnessing a perfect example of Special Forces' "silent death."

Sullivan glanced at the pilots who were still staring straight ahead as ordered. He then pulled Fitzwack behind the black curtain and drew it closed.

"Listen, Fitzwack, I need your help." Sullivan pulled his Special Operations ID out of the hidden pocket in his jacket and explained who he really was.

"You mean you want me to say *I* killed these guys?" the skinny man marveled after Sullivan laid it all out for him.

"If I take credit for the rescue, it'll blow my cover. And let's just say I've got bigger fish to fry."

"Well, sure, okay. If you say it's that important, I'll go along with it," Fitzwack agreed.

"Now you go tell the pilots they can head back for Beirut. I'll let the other passengers know it was you who saved us."

"Right," Fitzwack nodded, still a little dazed by the notion that he was going to be a hero. He went to pull back the curtain when Sullivan's huge paw on his shoulder stopped him.

"And one more thing, Fitzwack," Sullivan grunted under his breath.

"What's that?"

"Thanks."

JOIN THE *SPECIALIST* READERS' PANEL

Help us bring you more of the books you like by filling out this survey and mailing it in today.

1. Book Title: _____

   Book #: _____

2. Using the scale below, how would you rate this book on the following features? Please write in one rating from 0-10 for each feature in the spaces provided.

POOR		NOT SO GOOD		AVERAGE			GOOD		EXCEL-LENT	
0	1	2	3	4	5	6	7	8	9	10

RATING

Overall opinion of book . . . . _____

Plot/Story . . . . _____

Setting/Location . . . . _____

Writing Style . . . . _____

Dialogue . . . . _____

Suspense . . . . _____

Conclusion/Ending . . . . _____

Character Development . . . . _____

Hero . . . . _____

Scene on Front Cover . . . . _____

Colors of Front Cover . . . . _____

Back cover story outline . . . . _____

First page excerpts . . . . _____

3. How likely are you to buy another title in The *Specialist* series? (Circle one number on the scale below.)

DEFI-NITELY NOT BUY		PROB-ABLY NOT BUY		NOT SURE			PROB-ABLY BUY		DEFI-NITELY BUY	
0	1	2	3	4	5	6	7	8	9	10

4. Listed below are various Action Adventure lines. Rate only those you have read using the 0-10 scale below.

POOR		NOT SO GOOD		AVERAGE			GOOD		EXCEL-LENT	
0	1	2	3	4	5	6	7	8	9	10

RATING

Able Team .... _____
Death Merchant .... _____
Destroyer .... _____
Dirty Harry .... _____
Mack Bolan (Executioner) .... _____
Penetrator .... _____
Phoenix Force .... _____
Specialist .... _____
Survivalist .... _____
_____ .... _____
_____ .... _____

5. Where do you usually buy your books (check one or more):
( ) Bookstore   ( ) Discount Store
( ) Supermarket   ( ) Department Store
( ) Variety Store   ( ) Other: _____
( ) Drug Store

6. What are the names of two of your favorite magazines?
1) _____
2) _____

7. What is your age? _____   Sex: ( ) Male
                                          ( ) Female

8. Marital Status: Education:
( ) Single   ( ) Grammar school or less
( ) Married   ( ) Some high school
( ) Divorced   ( ) H.S. graduate
( ) Separated   ( ) 2 yrs. college
( ) Widowed   ( ) 4 yrs. college

If you would like to participate in future research projects, please complete the following:

PRINT NAME: _____
ADDRESS: _____
CITY: _____ STATE _____ ZIP _____
PHONE: ( ) _____

Thank you. Please send to: New American Library, Action Adventure Research Dept., 1633 Broadway, New York, New York 10019.